MAFIA DADDY

A Cinderella Adult Fairy Tale

JANE HENRY

SYNOPSIS:

Dante: She's Cinderella, but I'm no prince.

I'm son to the richest bastard in Vegas. Heir to the throne under one condition: *Find a wife, or I'll do it for you.*

And I found her. But every time she looks at me with those wide green eyes, her virgin body all curves and valleys, I know she is too good, too innocent.

I'll ruin her, but I can't let her go. *I lose my fucking mind when she calls me daddy.*

When the clock strikes midnight, the party's over. She better run, or my darkness will take over.

Gabriella: Meet me at midnight, he says.

My life is work. I promised my father I'd care for my step-mother and stepsisters. I don't have time for anything else.

Then I meet Dante. My Prince Charming. He brings my wildest, deepest fantasies to life. When he touches me, I forget the world. *I forget everything but him.*

When the clock strikes midnight, the party's over. Dante is hiding the truth from me, and his dark past could destroy everything.

PLEASE NOTE:

This is a work of fiction with adult themes, readers 18+ only, please.

Please do not distribute without written consent from the author.

ACKNOWLEDGMENTS

*Many thanks to the team that helped me build this book: Shannon from Shanoff Designs for a fantastic cover, Tease Book Graphics for amazing promo, Miranda for **everything** you did, hard-working proofers Jane and Alina, Editor Extraordinaire K.R. Nadelson, BFF beta Maisy, super fan Clubbers, and my dedicated reviewers!*

CHAPTER ONE

I smacked open the door to the expansive bathroom with my left hand, the right still aching as I curled it into a fist, careful not to let blood drip on the pristine floor. My shoes clicked on the tiles as I stalked to the sink and yanked the ivory handle. Every detail in this opulent room spoke of wealth and power, until I placed my hand under the running water, marring the perfection with splashes of blood.

Who was I kidding? The blood spoke of wealth and power, too.

I grabbed a towel, not caring that I ruined it with crimson stains as I wrapped it around my hand, until I'd staunched the flow of blood, gritting my teeth against the sting of fabric on raw wounds. With grim determination, in a routine that was sickeningly familiar, I opened the cabinet where we kept ample first aid supplies.

A few moments later, I'd covered up the evidence that I'd pounded the shit out of Charlie Beauregard. With my left hand, I cupped cool water into my palm and sipped it, before running my hand over my face and neck. I stood to my full height, and stared at myself hard in the mirror, seeing my mother's high cheekbones and my father's cold, calculating eyes. The sandy-colored beard and tattoos that edged along my neck, the incongruity defying my family's stature. I frowned at my dress shirt, expecting to see it stained with spattered blood, but to my surprise it was still clean.

I'd really let the son of a bitch have it. With an arsenal of weapons at my disposal, I could've used something to help me punish him. But no... I'd wanted my fist to cause the pain.

He hadn't even denied that he'd used the money he owed my father to buy women, women he then roughed up.

Bastard.

I cracked my neck and shifted my shoulders, trying to loosen up the tension bound in my body like a coiled snake. This was my job. The irony was, my father didn't even care that Beauregard beat up girls. I'd been sent to teach him a lesson because of his defiance against the family. He owed money. He didn't pay up. Therefore, he was punished. A simple equation.

Knowing he was a sick bastard only made my job easier. I breathed in, my chest expanding as I stared at myself in the mirror, then exhaled slowly, when my phone buzzed.

Your father will see you now.

I smirked. The hell he would.

I'd go to his office to update him. But see me? He never truly did.

I gazed out the window overlooking the Vegas Strip and took another pull from my beer, doing my best to ignore the man sitting beside me. I wanted to hurt him, and I couldn't. It didn't matter that he was my father. He was

Antonio Villanova, mafia lord of Sin City, and he owned every single glittering detail below us... the casinos, the restaurants, all the surrounding shops.

He fucking owned the air.

"Are you listening to me?" he asked, in that tone I'd learned to obey since I was crawling on the floor eating Cheerios. The sharpness sent a shiver down my spine, my hand gripping my beer bottle more tightly as I fought to control conditioned anger.

"Yeah, Dad. I heard you. You want me to find a wife."

"Dante, look at me." His voice had grown dangerously low. I inhaled before I turned to face him, steeling myself for the disapproval I was sure to see written in his stern features. When I turned to face him, a bit of the rage that burned within me softened. He didn't look disapproving, or even angry anymore.

He looked afraid.

"Well? What's on your mind?"

He sat, as thin and fragile as I'd ever seen him. The deep-set dark eyes that once burned with power now lacked fire, his jowls hiding his strong, clean-shaven jaw. My eyes drifted down to his signature black dress shirt, unfastened at the collar, the tie hanging loose about his neck like a noose. "I'm old, Dante. And I won't be here forever. You know how this works. If you don't find a wife, your cousin Emilio will get everything, and it will kill me to see my legacy handed over to my brother's family. Do you hear me? *Kill me,* not to mention what it would do to your mother.*"

He'd survived shoot-outs, car chases, three stints in jail, and more attempts on his life than I could keep track of. And now he was telling me it would kill him if I didn't marry? Hell.

"Yeah, I know. I get it. I know what you want me to do." I

turned away from my father, hardly able to stomach looking at him anymore, and found myself gazing back out the window at the flashing lights and hordes of people far, far below. I spotted a woman with her hand outstretched, gesturing wildly to a man twice her size, and I wondered what her story was. Had he looked at another girl? Forgotten her birthday? Acted like an asshole?

How *did* normal people live their lives?

"What *you* don't get is that you don't find wives the way you find, say, your favorite bottle of Merlot or an unblemished Lamborghini. You can't just go shopping and *buy* one for God's sake."

His low, sadistic chuckle startled me. It was the same sound I heard before he ordered a hit, and it indicated anything but humor.

"My son, you are naïve. So goddamned naïve."

I clenched my fist around my bottle and took another swig. The beer had grown warm, but I gulped it down to swallow the bile in my throat.

He was right. It had been a naïve comment. Antonio Villanova bought whatever he fucking wanted. Women were no exception.

"You see, son," he continued, and I could hear his chair creak back and knew without looking at him that he was sitting with his fingertips pressed together, assuming the role of patriarch, the wise, all-knowing King of Vegas. "You may have forgotten that in our family, we value tradition. We are, after all, the longest line of Villanovas on the West Coast. One of the reasons I've worked so hard at upholding my legacy is so that our family traditions don't become diluted. So we don't allow paupers, loafers, or ingrates into our stock. You know this, son."

He spoke with such warmth, it was hard to fathom that

he spewed hatred and venom in his words, but I knew this mantra well.

Traditional values.

Family loyalty.

Longstanding traditions.

"Yeah. I get it. I do." I ran a finger along the length of the side of the bottle and watched in amusement as the guy being publicly lectured by his woman reached for her, pulling her close to him in a hug, and she swiped at her eyes with the back of her hand.

I shook my head. If she were mine, I'd blister her ass for yelling at me in public.

My father's words rang in the quiet of the room as I stared down at the strangers.

"*Do* you, Dante?"

I turned to look at him again, and as I had suspected, he sat with his fingertips pressed together, his eyes fixed on me. "Do you really know what's at stake here, son?"

I swallowed. I had a mother, still, to look out for. My dad commanded an army, and though our public persona as legitimate Vegas real estate magnates was well-known, everyone knew who we really were. The line of Villanovas populated the streets of our city like stars in the night sky. We were large, we were powerful, and we were unstoppable.

My father continued. "So what will it be, Dante? Will you find a wife, or will I do it for you?"

I swallowed the last dregs of my beer before I stood, clenching the bottle in my hand.

Hating myself for what I was about to say, I threw the bottle into the trashcan by the door so hard it shattered into shards on impact.

"I'll do it," I said, slamming the door behind me before he had a chance to reply.

*T*wisted off my tie, and tossed it in a pile with my suit jacket and dress shirt, shoving them all in a duffel bag. Yeah, my mother paid five grand for this suit, and it was custom-made, but I didn't give a shit. I'd have it cleaned or pressed or whatever the fuck I needed to do. I needed to be someone I wasn't, for just a little while... Or maybe the truth was, I needed to shrug off the facade and be who I *really* was. I locked the car. I wouldn't be driving it tonight.

I'd skimmed down to my worn Levi's and a threadbare *Guns N' Roses* t-shirt I'd had for years, and felt my adrenaline surge as I took out the keys to my bike. I needed to ride, feel the wind at my back, to shake off the hold my father had on me. Spread my wings a bit, even if it was just for the night.

God, it felt good to swing my leg over the side of my bike and lean into it, feeling that heady rush of impending freedom as I gripped the familiar handlebars. I revved the engine, and the power rumbled beneath me. I had no idea where I was going, but I knew it had to be to a place that really *did* sleep, that had streetlights that went on and off, and stars that twinkled in a real nighttime sky. A place where I could breathe in fresh air and see green grass for miles.

I rode for a full hour, until the sun began to set and the wind picked up, though the air was still as oppressive as ever. May in Vegas was hot as fucking Hades, no matter what time of day. But the breeze felt nice.

Maybe I'd find a place to stay for the night, where no one knew who I was or who my father was. Maybe I'd stay for a week.

Maybe I wouldn't go back.

I only entertained the idea briefly, though. I knew I had to go back.

Just as I was about to pull over to look at my phone and find a place to stay, I saw her.

Jesus Christ, she was beautiful.

Long, blonde hair, so light it was nearly white, hung to her waist in waves, and when she turned her face toward me, I could see her high cheekbones, perfect, full lips the color of strawberries, a willowy figure of grace and gentility. She held a purse in one hand, and her phone in the other, and as I pulled over toward her, she smiled at me, a full-on smile revealing a pair of gorgeous dimples. I was close enough to see her eyes now, a pretty green framed with long, dark lashes, set beneath delicately arched brows. I cut the engine.

"Oh, thank goodness," she said, in a sweet, clear voice that stirred something primal inside of me. "I was afraid I'd have to walk the whole way practically barefoot, and my phone is dead. Do you have a phone, mister?" She blinked at me with those fetching green eyes and I wanted to kiss her.

I'd never wanted to kiss a woman. I'd only ever wanted to fuck them senseless. This girl was... different.

"Of course," I said, but as I put the kickstand of my bike down, I felt a twinge of protective anger surge within me. "But before I give you my phone, you need to tell me why a young girl like you is all alone this far from civilization. What the hell happened to you?"

She looked down bashfully and twisted her toe in the loose gravel by the side of the road. "Well..." she began. "I *was* here with my sisters. You see, they're not *really* my sisters but step-sisters, and we had plans tonight to go to a concert. Only problem was, Violet had a boyfriend and Elenora had a date, and we could barely squeeze into the car. We made it work, but then they decided they needed more room because one of their friends could come after all."

"So... they kicked you out?"

"Ummm... yes... pretty much. And, well, I missed the bus

I was planning to take, and it appears my charger never *did* charge my phone like it was supposed to." She shrugged. "And then my flip-flop broke." She gestured to the cheap, broken flip-flop and sighed. "And that's about it. I'm stranded because I'm stupid and naïve and ill-prepared."

I shook my head, handing her the phone. If she were mine, she wouldn't be allowed to call herself stupid. And she sure as hell never would've been out here alone with an unreliable phone and no method of getting home, wearing cheap flip-flops no less. Who was I kidding? If she were mine, I wouldn't let her out of my fucking sight.

I grunted as she looked in surprise at my phone. It was showy, crazy expensive, and big. Whatever. People had snazzy phones in Vegas, and I wouldn't make any excuses.

"Not sure how to use this," she murmured. I took it from her, and my hand brushed hers, just the barest of touches that sent a bolt of electricity through me. I blinked, momentarily taken aback. She smelled *so* fucking good too, like caramel and vanilla.

"Here," I grumbled. "Push this and dial."

"Thank you, Mister..." she halted, not knowing my name.

"Dante. You can call me Dante." Dante Villanova. Would she know my name? I waited, looking for signs that she knew me, recognized my identity.

"Thank you, Mister Dante."

I chuckled. *Cute.* "No, just Dante," I said.

She nodded her head eagerly. "I am *so* grateful, you have no idea."

I warmed at that, shoving my hands in my pockets, and covered up my pleasure by being gruff with her. "Make the call."

Her hands trembled a bit as she dialed, then held the phone up to her ear. Leaning in, she put her hand over the mouthpiece. "I'm just calling my stepmother," she whispered, her wide green eyes looking into mine.

"Of course," I said, suddenly feeling magnanimous. "Whatever you need."

She smiled widely and mouthed *thank you*, then spoke into the phone.

"Oh, hello, Mabel. How are you? How is little Ellie faring?"

What the fuck? She was making small talk? I frowned at her, but she ignored me and kept jabbering. "Oh, I'm *so* glad. I was afraid she'd caught that nasty flu that was going around. Yes, I wasn't working tonight. The girls and I were going to a concert, but we ran into a bit of trouble, you see. Oh, yes. I *know*. Yes, you're right! Ah-ha. Mmm. Well, that's true," she said.

I touched her arm, and she jumped as if she just remembered I was there. Covering the mouthpiece of the phone with her hand, she leaned over to me. "Just a minute. I'm so sorry, but it's important I engage her in conversation and not just ignore the fact that she had a little girl ill last evening. Am I using up your cell phone minutes, or taking up your time?" Her green eyes blinked up at me, and I almost smiled at her.

People still had phones with minutes on them? "Well, no," I grumbled. It wasn't about my minutes or my time. The girl needed help.

She nodded. "Good. Thank you!" She removed her hand from the mouthpiece and spoke into the phone. "Oh, that's *so* true. I understand. I believe in good, old-fashioned remedies, too!"

Old-fashioned remedies, my ass. I'd give her a good, old-fashioned remedy right over my knee if she didn't hurry it up already. I crossed my arms and gave her the sternest look I could muster.

It did the trick. Her jaw dropped and her voice rose in pitch as she spoke. "Mabel? Please fetch Agatha, will you please? I must speak to her at once."

She had such a funny, quaint way of speaking. It was adorable. But then, her face fell, and just like everything else about her, her features betrayed her feelings. "Oh, I'm sorry to hear that," she said with a sigh. "No, no need to bother her then. I'll talk to her when I get home. I'm sure I'll find a way. Goodnight." She hung up the phone and handed it to me, not meeting my eyes.

"And?" I asked, tucking the phone into my back pocket.

"Agatha, my stepmother, has a client she's meeting with," she said, "and gave strict orders not to be interrupted."

God, this girl needed to be taken care of. She should not have been stranded on the side of the road where any crazy fuck could pick her up, and use her.

Like me.

It seemed fate was working its magic tonight.

"Alright, then," I said. "You ever ridden on the back of a bike?"

She blinked up at me again. "Excuse me?"

"A bike, honey. Like my motorcycle." I gestured toward the seat for emphasis. "You ever ridden on one?"

She shook her head from side to side with wide, innocent eyes, her lips parted like a child on Christmas morning. "*No,*" she breathed. "*Never. Oh my God.* You're going to *rescue* me?"

And before I could respond she legit squealed out loud, bouncing on the tips of her toes and clapping her hands. She practically leapt at me, throwing her arms around my neck and squeezing tight. On impulse, I hugged her back, folding her into my embrace. She was tiny, and so fragile, and she fit as if she were meant for me. I would see her home safely.

A little voice, unbidden, whispered in my ear. *She could be the one. The one that you need.*

But just as quickly as the voice surfaced, I shoved it away.

No. Fucking. *Way* would I bring a girl like this anywhere near my father, and even if I wanted to, I could tell with one glance at her she didn't fit the bill. She was too poor, for one. Too young.

And way, *way* too innocent.

I let her go before I did something stupid, like kiss her breathless. She threw her bag over her shoulder and tried to leap straight onto the bike.

"Whoa, now, honey. Easy does it. I hold the bike steady for you, and you get on, you hear? You could hurt yourself climbing on that big thing all by yourself." Something about her made me feel like a knight or something, like I was someone who had to take care of her. I held the bike steady as she swung a leg up. She was so cute, her legs dangling on either side, her eyes bright and shining at me.

"Yes! Let's do this! Let's go! Wooohooooo!"

I laughed out loud, the sound so unfamiliar to my own ears, it nearly startled me. "Hold onto my waist," I instructed, as I swung my leg over the bike in front of her. "Hey, do you have a name?"

"Gabriella," she answered.

"Hang on tight, Gabriella," I said over my shoulder, gunning the engine to life. My laughter died into the wind along with her shrieks and hoots and hollers. I wasn't sure where I'd go or where I'd take her, but I'd enjoy every minute of this while it lasted.

"Excuse me? Do you have to take me right home? Or can we go for a teensy little ride first?"

I grinned. "We can do whatever you want, Gabriella." The night was young. Magical, even. It would not hold us back. Yeah, I was going to rescue her, this little, blonde-haired, green-eyed girl I'd found stranded on the side of the road. For one night, I'd pretend I wasn't me. Make sure she was safe. Pretend to be the good guy.

Just for tonight, I'd be her fucking Prince Charming.

CHAPTER TWO

Oh my God! I was on the back of a motorcycle, and it wasn't one of those little, puny ones either. This one was so big and powerful that when it roared to life beneath me, I felt like a little girl riding on a carousel. Dante drove *fast,* and I loved that. The pavement beneath the wheels flew past as I gripped him for dear life. My arms held tight around his waist, and I could feel his taut muscles beneath the thin fabric of the t-shirt he wore.

If my step sisters could see me now! This guy was *hot,* big and broad-shouldered, with a scruffy, blondish-brown beard, dark brown eyes, and tattoos that crept along his neck and up his arms. Whenever he looked at me, I felt all shivery inside. His eyes held something I couldn't decipher. It wasn't... sinister. But it wasn't safe, either.

Still, I trusted him.

Then again, I trusted most people. I really couldn't help it. Life was better that way, maybe.

We rode for a while without speaking. We couldn't have said anything if we tried, the sound of the engine and wind whipping past us were too loud. The night grew cold, and I knew I'd have to get back home eventually. But tonight I'd enjoy myself.

Dark clouds had rolled in.

"Gonna get some rain," Dante said, in his deep, raspy voice. "You want to get something to eat?"

My stomach growled traitorously. I had no money with me, and could not ask for a handout.

"No, thank you," I said, as he stopped the bike and held it steady. He looked over his shoulder at me.

"Well, I'm starving and I don't wanna be caught on the back of this bike when the rain comes," he said. "Come in with me and have a drink?"

This was like... a date?

Like a real date that people had.

I'd never been on a date.

My heart pitter-pattered and I could only nod dumbly.

I would never forget this night.

"Sure," I said, as if he hadn't just asked me on my first date. "I'd love a chocolate milk or something."

His eyes crinkled around the edges and he smiled at me, in a way that made my heart flutter rapidly against my chest. "Chocolate milk?" he asked, putting the kickstand of his bike down. "You want chocolate milk?"

I straightened and stretched my arms, yawning. I was so tired, having been up before the sun rose and walking all that way until he picked me up.

Then I remembered I had no money. "Actually, maybe just water," I said, following him toward a little diner. He made some kind of grunty noise, as he held the door open for me.

A middle-aged waitress with her hair piled up in a bun and large, oval-shaped glasses perched on her nose giving her the appearance of an owl, watched us walk in with her mouth hanging wide open. Why the heck did she do that? We didn't look *that* weird or out-of-place, did we?

"Table for two, please," Dante rumbled. The woman picked up the menus, dropped them on the floor, then picked them up again with trembling hands. How odd.

"Yes, of course," she said. "Right this way." She led us to a little table in the back with black spindly chairs and a plastic red and white checkered tablecloth. She placed our menus down. "Special's on the front, but we're out of apple pie. You can have anything else you'd like, though, and straight away."

"Thank you," Dante said, pulling out a chair for me and pointing for me to sit.

I nodded my thanks and sat, scooting my chair up closer to the table.

Something smelled really yummy, and my stomach growled again, but I would not open the menu. "Just a water for me, please," I said, as he took his seat. He raised a heavy, dark blond brow at me and pursed his lips.

"Why just water? You're not hungry?"

My mouth watered as the smell of French fries wafted through the air.

I couldn't lie.

"Well, I'm starving," I said. "I just... I forgot my money, and don't want to be obliged to you any more than I already am. But if you... if you get me something to eat I will repay you." I was so hungry.

The humor in his eyes fled, then, and he sobered. It was a little scary, actually.

He pointed a stern finger to the menu. "Pick out what you want," he ordered in his raspy voice.

I looked down shyly, pleased, and a little bashful. "Okay. Yes, I will."

As I looked over the menu, it occurred to me he looked vaguely familiar, but I couldn't quite place him. Was he a customer where I worked? There were so many people who came there, I never could identify everyone I saw. Or did I know him from somewhere else?

He folded his menu and sat back in his chair. "Pick something out?"

"I'll have the chicken tender platter, please," I said.

His lips twitched. "And chocolate milk?"

I nodded eagerly. "Yes, please."

The waitress took our orders moments later, and placed a plastic basket of bread on the table. As we waited he leaned back in his chair, his large, muscular arms crossed over his t-shirt. I tried to observe him without him noticing, but how could he not? We were the only people in the restaurant. I distracted myself with a piece of bread.

He looked at me as I stared, and I quickly looked away again.

"So, Gabriella," he said. "Let me get this straight. You went to a concert because your sister got free tickets, and you wanted to go. But then one of the friends who was supposed to meet you decided he wanted the ride, so you were ousted? Seriously?"

"Well. Yeah. Something like that." The truth was, I was rarely allowed to join them.

He chewed thoughtfully on his own piece of bread now, and my eyes fell to his bandaged hand.

"Did you hurt yourself?" I asked.

He shrugged. "It's nothing. Hurt my hand a bit working on my bike. So, it seems your sisters are not very loyal." I didn't answer, because I wasn't exactly sure how I was supposed to respond. "Meanwhile," he muttered under his breath. "Loyalty is just about all my family has."

"Well, that's good at least," I said helpfully, as I took a sip of my drink. "Loyalty is important."

He looked at me without blinking as he chewed his bread,

and after a moment of awkward silence, he looked away and changed the subject.

Well then.

"So what about your family? Do you have any other siblings?"

I shook my head. "No. My father died three years ago in an accident, and my mother died when I was just a little girl. I was their only child."

"I'm sorry to hear about your losses," he offered gruffly, and as I glanced over at him, I could read sympathy in his eyes.

"Thank you. I miss them." My throat tightened a bit, so I took a sip of my milk, swallowing down the lump that had lodged there. "And you?" I asked. "Do you have a father and mother? Well, I mean, everyone has a father and a mother, or they wouldn't exist. It's a silly question, really. But what I mean is, are your parents still alive?" He stared at me in surprise as I stammered on like a freshman on her first date with the varsity football captain. "I mean, they, um, didn't die?" Oh, God, what an idiot. "Did they?" I squeaked. "Are they alive?"

He smiled at me, his dark brown eyes lighting up his otherwise somber expression. "Yeah," he said. "At least they were when I saw them an hour ago."

"Oh my gosh," I said, embarrassed.

"Hey," he said. "I'm just teasing you. Yeah, my parents are alive. They sell property, and I manage that for them." He said it nonchalantly, but he didn't look in my eyes when he did.

Weird.

It was that moment the waitress chose to bring our food over, and I was so grateful I could bury myself in my food and not embarrass myself anymore.

"Thank you," I said. The smell of the fries and chicken

had my stomach clenching in hunger. "These look amazing. Seriously. They look really good. God, I'm famished."

Dante took his burger and we both ate in silence for a while. Finally, he put his food down and looked at me.

"Gabriella," he said. "What would you have done if I hadn't found you?"

I didn't answer right away. It was a fair question, and one I'd been pondering while I'd walked along the side of the road in just my broken flip flops. "Honestly, I don't know," I admitted. "I would've maybe... kept walking or something until another kind soul stopped to let me make a call on their phone, I guess."

"Alone. Without a way to get back?"

"You know, I'd have found a way. Everything always works out in the end."

"Does it?" he asked quietly, his eyes growing strangely serious.

"Well, yes. I think so, anyway," I said.

"Not sure this burger worked out," he muttered with a grimace, as he placed it back on his plate. I laughed.

"Here, have some chicken," I said, offering him mine, but he shook his head and continued to look at me with curiosity.

"So what do you do for work?"

"I'm a waitress and restaurant manager," I said with a smile. "In Vegas. I wait tables."

He smiled. "Yeah? Well that's a respectable job, Gabriella," he said. "And I bet it keeps you busy. What do you do in your free time?"

"Free time is pretty much nonexistent," I explained. "I used to do things like paint, or craft, or sew, but it seems these days that all I do is work. I guess it's maybe just the way things are when you hit adulthood." My eyes hit his. "What about you?"

He shook his head. "I don't really want to talk about me,"

he said brusquely. "Back to you. So can you tell me a little more about your parents?"

Well, that was a little weird, but I didn't comment. He was buying me dinner, so the least I could do was cooperate.

"Have you seen any ketchup?" I asked. My fries were nice and piping hot and just a little salty.

He smirked, removing an enormous bottle of ketchup from behind the dessert menu, he opened it, squeezing some out onto my plate for me.

"Thank you," I said, swiping a fry through the ketchup and popping it in my mouth.

He watched me eat, not touching his own food, and I squirmed a bit. Finally, he spoke again.

"So, you think chowing down on these fries is gonna get you out of answering my question?" he asked. Though his eyes danced, teasing me, his voice held a hard edge that made me want to please him.

"What was your question again?" I asked him, stalling. I didn't want to talk about my parents. It was a sad story for me, one I didn't feel like revisiting when I was in the middle of this totally surreal night, with a hot guy, eating fries and chicken tenders in a little hole-in-the-wall diner.

"Your parents?" he prodded, taking another reluctant bite of his burger.

"Oh. Right. Well, like I said, my dad passed away. He died in a shooting downtown a few years back. Got on the wrong side of a robbery. It was a real tragedy, to be honest," I said, speaking quickly and not looking at him as I chewed a few more fries and swallowed them down with my drink. "I... I miss him a lot. He was a good man, and I learned a lot from him."

My hand shook a little, then. Most days, I was fine, going along with whatever task was in front of me. My stepmother kept me busy as heck, managing the restaurant. I oversaw most things. But it was what I did, what I had to do to earn my keep. "My dad left me with nothing," I explained. "It wasn't supposed to be that way. But when my stepmother married him, she became executor of his will, and everything he owned went to her. She says that he declared bankruptcy before he died and left me penniless."

Why was I sharing my heart with this man I didn't know from Adam?

As usual, though, I didn't stop. I couldn't. Once I started talking, I had a hard time reining myself in.

"My mom was an entertainer. A singer. She had the most beautiful voice you could imagine, Dante. Just beautiful. The voice of an angel, my father would say." My food lay forgotten as I recounted my story to him. "And she was so good. So very, very good. She never asked for anything for herself, and she always met the needs of everyone around her. I wish I could be as good."

Dante's eyes narrowed ever so slightly. "Who says you aren't?" he asked softly.

I shook my head. "I'm not," I said to my plate, not meeting his eyes. "I couldn't be." If he met my stepmother, maybe he'd understand why...

Dante didn't need to know all that, though.

"So yeah, my mom is sadly gone, but I learned a lot from her. I wish someday to be as good as she was."

He nodded slowly, picked up his burger and took a bite, then swallowed it before replying. "A noble goal, Gabriella," he said. "To strive to be good, like people we admire. I like that. Everyone should have someone in their lives who inspires them to be a better person." His gaze met mine, and I squirmed a bit.

"They should," I whispered, and for some weird reason, I wanted to cry. I hadn't talked about my family situation to anyone in years... or had I ever? I was far too busy working to have any friends. It felt oddly cathartic talking to Dante about my parents, because after tonight, I don't think I'll ever see him again.

"So what about you?" I asked. "Do you have any brothers or sisters?"

He sat back in his chair and swallowed the mouthful of food he was chewing before replying. He took a long pull from his Coke, and eyed me thoughtfully before continuing. "No. Just my mother, whom I love, and my father, who can be downright ruthless."

I frowned, and took another sip of my milk before wiping my mouth with my napkin. "Well... I'm not sure ruthlessness is an admirable trait."

His jaw tightened. "It's not."

"Hmm. Well," I said, trying to find something positive to say. "It seems that your family is... an interesting sort?"

He laughed, a deep-barreled laugh that made me shiver for some reason, reminding me that although he was strong and sexy, he was dangerous.

"An interesting sort is a nice way to put it," he said. "I like you, Gabriella. Do you ever have anything bad to say about anyone?"

I shrugged. "Well," I said as honestly as I could. "I don't like when people are unkind, or greedy, or take advantage of others. But I don't like to think of sad things, so no, I'd prefer even then not to say anything bad about people. I'm just happier that way, I guess."

"Makes sense," he said. "And I get it. Not the way I do things, but then again, I wouldn't recommend you do anything the way I do it."

What was wrong with him? What troubled him? He frowned, and snapped open the dessert menu.

"You want some dessert?" he asked, and I nodded eagerly.

"You were a good girl, and ate your dinner, and good girls who eat dinner get dessert."

My belly turned to mush at hearing him call me a *good girl*.

Oh, God. I *was* a good girl. So why, then, did I feel a tingling between my thighs, and heat rising in my chest at his words? I decided to change the subject.

"Dante, did you notice that dessert menu easily has three or four dozen different options? We maybe should have noticed that before we ordered our food." I stared at his half-eaten burger. "Maybe next time, we just order dessert and skip the meal altogether."

His lips twitched and my heart twisted once more. "I think that's a very good idea," he said, but there was sadness in his eyes, and I realized the error of my ways. How foolish I'd been.

How could there possibly be a next time?

"I'd love a piece of cherry pie. Do they do á la mode? And why do they call it á la mode anyway? Is *mode* French for ice cream? Why would a language have fancy words like *enchantée* and *patisserie*, but then have something like mode for something as delectable as ice cream?" He shook his head.

"You're something else," he said. "But yeah, honey, it means with ice cream. So tell me, do you want it á la mode or not?"

"Yes, of course. Please," I tacked on, feeling suddenly bashful.

He smiled again. Maybe he wasn't so scary. "Good girl."

It took me by surprise, being called a good girl again, but it did wonderful, surprising things to me. I felt shy and happy and admittedly turned on. I wanted to continue to be his good girl... but how? I couldn't.

I needed to get home. I needed to pretend I'd never met this man before.

I would never forget him, but I needed him to forget me.

CHAPTER THREE

I watched in rapt fascination as she ate her cherry pie. Her green eyes were alight as she talked of so many things—her favorite books and movies, interspersed with sweet little questions trying to get me to uphold my end of the conversation. But I wouldn't answer her questions, and kept redirecting the conversation back to her. I wanted to know everything about her. What made her happy, or sad, or hopeful? Her hopes, her dreams, and her fears. I wanted it all, every bit of it.

I'd had everything handed to me on a silver platter, since before I could remember. Even now, I had plastic in my wallet that could buy me a house or a yacht or anything else I wanted. My dad was a filthy rich billionaire, and I'd already amassed my own fortune. It had come at a price, though. I'd seen terrible, wicked things in my thirty years. I'd *done* terrible, wicked things.

Something in me longed for the type of goodness that was born of a pure heart. It was in Gabriella's eyes, in her speech. She was good, this girl... this beguiling young woman.

"Oh, that was delicious, Dante," she said, wiping her mouth. "It really was. I'm so sorry you didn't like your burger, though. Perhaps the cook was having a bad night or something."

"Doesn't matter," I said. "I'm glad you liked your meal. Now let's get going."

Her eyes clouded a bit, and something in me yearned to make her happy again. "Sure," she said. "Is it time to go back already?"

Ah. She thought it was time to go home. Sweet girl.

I looked out the window, then, at the dark, ominous clouds that had rolled in while we were eating. "Not so sure about that," I said. The one major downside of riding a motorcycle was the severe lack of protection in case of a storm, and in Vegas flash floods happened on the regular. I kept a leather jacket it my saddlebag that would protect me, but what did Gabriella have? I'd make her wear mine, of course, but it would be so big on her I wasn't sure how much shelter it would offer.

"So how am I going to repay you, Prince Charming? You bought me dinner and rescued me from dead-cell-phone, broken-flip-flop hell. You bought me the most delicious cherry pie and sacrificed your own comfort eating a subpar burger in a diner in the middle of nowhere. So how do I make this up to you?" She smiled up at me, and something in me roared to life, something I hadn't felt in so long, the feeling was completely foreign to me.

Hope.

"You don't need to repay me, babe," I said, waving my ‌‍nd. "I needed the distraction tonight, to be honest."

‍‍‍de brow furrowed and she pursed her lips.

ow. I can't just be a *moocher*."

a's pride was getting in the way.

a kiss," I said, before I could stop the

words, before I knew better than to ask for it. I just wanted a chaste kiss. I wouldn't hurt her, or take advantage of her, or use her. Just one little kiss.

"A kiss?" she whispered, her eyes lighting up but looking away just as quickly. "Well, I suppose it's a small price to pay," she said with a shrug.

And then she stood up on her tiptoes as she faced me, steadying herself by placing her hands on my shoulders for balance, and she placed the sweetest little kiss on my cheek. "There," she said with a giggle. "There's your kiss."

I wanted to ravish her, to make her mine, take her mouth and give her a kiss she'd never fucking forget.

"You kissed my cheek?" I drawled. "You call that repayment?"

I was just teasing her. But her eyes widened and she grew quiet, and before I knew what was happening, her head tilted to the side, her lips met mine, and magic happened.

Fucking magic.

At the touch of her lips my cock hardened, my muscles tensed, and I deepened the kiss. Her knees dipped and she moaned a bit, and I lost myself in her. I kissed her as if tonight was our last night, and tomorrow would never come. Like she was my savior. Like this was her first kiss, and I'd make sure she never fucking forgot it. Finally, reluctantly, I pulled away before I did something I regretted, like tear her clothes right off her porcelain skin and fuck her up against the wall.

"Going back might be dangerous now," I mused, as I looked around the little strip mall where we stood. A flash of lightning lit up the sky behind us like an omen, and Gabriella shivered. I stood taller and lifted one of my arms to draw her against me, to protect her, the instinct so strong the move was unconscious, involuntary even.

"I don't know what we should do," Gabriella murmured,

tugging on her lower lip with her teeth and lowering her eyes shyly, snuggling closer. "My stepmother won't miss me until the morning, and I don't want to go back, Dante. Not now. And is it even safe to ride with... whatever is coming?"

As I looked around I noticed the restaurant was closing, the shades drawn and the fluorescent lights that promised "hot pie" and "best fries in town" vanishing as we watched. To the right of the diner was a little convenience store, and to the right of that, a strip of pavement that led to a looming building in the distance. I squinted my eyes and looked. Was it what I thought it was? I tilted my head and read the white script against the green background on the awning.

King's Crown Hotel.

"We could head over there for a bit," I said, pointing to the awning in the distance. "You know, get out of the rain."

"Well," she said before she blinked, her large green eyes reflecting something more than what they showed just a minute before. Her cheeks flushed. "That was... that was my first kiss, Dante, and I have to say it was a really damn good one. And I don't think I'm quite myself yet."

I barked out a laugh. I'd known this girl for less than a day, and she undid me. She beamed up at me.

First kiss? "That was not *your* first kiss, was it?" she asked innocently.

My laughter died and I shook my head. *Jesus.*

"No, babe. It wasn't my first kiss." It *was* a first, though it would be hard to explain what made it so... It was my first taste of innocence. The first time I kissed a girl and cared if she liked it.

"Hey," I said, brushing her hair out of her eyes with the back of my finger. "We're in for quite a storm."

"Are we?" she asked, and to my surprise, she tilted her head to the side and sobered. "This night is something different, Dante." A crash of thunder overhead interrupted her, and it was followed by a flash of lightning that lit up the sky. She shrieked, and I gathered her close.

"I'm afraid," she said, and as I held her against me, the first splatter of a raindrop hit my cheek, cold and wet.

"Afraid of what? Of the storm?"

Her eyes were closed now, and her face paled as she nodded her head. She looked like she was gonna throw up or something. "I hate thunderstorms," she whispered, right before another slash of lightning came, along with a deafening crash of thunder, and the rain began. She screamed at the flash in the sky, and held onto me with a death-like grip, her fingers grasping my shirt as if to anchor herself to safety. My gut clenched at her whimper. I held her as she rocked a bit, and I knew then that I had to get her to safety, had to get her out of this storm. I knew if the thunder and lightning were this close to one another, we were in the eye of the storm, and it definitely wasn't safe. And the girl was fucking terrified.

Why? What had happened to her to make her scared like this? The brave, happy woman from a few minutes ago had dissolved into a shaking, petrified little girl.

"Come with me," I said, as yet another string of lighting and thunder lit up the sky, the rain coming down in such torrents I had to shout for her to hear me. We were soaked through within seconds as I made my way to the entrance. I tried to pull her along, as she didn't seem capable of walking on her own, and was ready to swing her up in my arms and fucking carry her the rest of the way if I had to. She didn't budge, just wrapped her arms around herself and rocked back and forth as the rain poured down around us.

"Gabriella," I yelled above the roar of the storm. "Move! Go! We need to get out of here," but she could hardly hear me. I grasped her upper arm, spun her around, and smacked her ass, hard.

"Move!"

That got her attention. She blinked as if waking from a dream, and when I pulled her along with me, she trotted to keep up. The door was shut tight with the wind pushing it closed, but I yanked it hard, and breathed a sigh of relief when the door finally opened. "Go!" I ordered. "Get your ass in there!"

When we were both safe inside, I pulled the door shut behind us. It grew suddenly quiet.

She looked up at me, her sopping wet hair hanging about her face in strands, her top clinging to her chest, her jeans sodden. A little trail of black mascara pooled around the edges of her eyes. She stood in silence, but when another clap of thunder boomed, she shut her eyes and tucked her chin against her chest. I grabbed her arm and pulled her along with me, not harshly but firmly enough that she wouldn't freeze up again.

A tall boy with straggly brown hair and huge, round glasses blinked up at us from behind a desk. I could tell from the minute he looked at me that he knew who I was, and I pushed down the anger that twisted in my gut. I fantasized briefly—I'd grab him by the front of his shirt, shove him across the desk, and growl into his ear that if he told her who I was I'd fucking kill him. But as soon as the violent image came into my head, I pushed it away again. God, was it *his* fault that people knew me? That I had a reputation that preceded me? That people were afraid of me?

For just tonight, I was not Dante Villanova, Mafia Prince and ruler-in-line to the Villanova Dynasty.

I was just Dante.

"Room for two," I ordered. "And I need one with two beds, please."

"Y-yes, Mr. Vi—"

I held up a finger to stop him and shook my head sharply, using one of my go-to fake names. "Ringwald," I said. "Mister Ringwald."

He blinked. "Certainly, Mister Ringwald. But I-I'm sorry to tell you, we have no more rooms with two beds. They're all taken."

What the fuck?

"What do you mean they're all taken?" How the hell did that happen?

He shrugged. "Wedding last night down the road," he said. "All we have left is the master suite on the very top floor. But that suite is our most private, Mister Vi-Ringwald. You'll, um, not be disturbed, and it comes with free continental breakfast."

I glanced over at Gabriella, who had her arms wrapped around herself, rocking back and forth, eyes shut tight. Jesus, she was still terrified. The thunder clapped ahead, and she emitted a little scream.

"Fine," I muttered. "Whatever. Just get me a room."

"Yes, sir," he said, taking the credit card I offered him, the one with the fake name on it that we used for times like this. He stared at it, and I leaned across the counter and whispered to him. "Run the card. Stop talking to me. And get me the fucking room. Believe me, the card will go through." I could've charged the whole fucking hotel on it and it would run through. *Jesus.*

He ran it, his hand trembling as he handed me paperwork to sign. "Checkout is at noon, and breakfast begins at 7 a.m.," he said. "To the left is the entrance to the pool, sir, and down the hall—"

"Give me the damn key." I sounded like a high school bully who was about to shake him down for his lunch money, but I needed to get the girl alone, to safety, where I could hold her in my arms and get her to stop trembling.

I needed to take care of her.

He handed me the key, I took Gabriella's hand, and I whisked her out of the lobby and to the elevator. But when I pushed the button, she shook her head from side to side.

Fuck.

"No elevator," she pleaded "No elevators, please. I hate them. And it's a storm. If we got stuck, and the electricity went out—please, no elevator."

What had happened to this girl? Why was she so scared? Who had hurt her?

How would I make them fucking pay?

"Ok, honey," I said. "No elevator. We're a few floors up. Can you walk?"

She stumbled behind me as I led her to the stairs, and I looked down. Her stupid broken flip-flop. "Take 'em off," I ordered, pointing to her shoes, and she obeyed, padding by my side barefoot, but when I opened the door to the stair-well, I cringed. It was littered with scattered pieces of broken glass. The stairs were filthy. Thunder rumbled again, and she screamed out loud. I bent, wrapped my arms around the back of her legs and scooped her up into my arms, letting the door shut hard behind us. Her arms looped around my neck, and her head fell to my chest. Though we were soaking wet, the warmth of her head on my chest made my insides curl a bit, and I wished that the flight up to our room was a lot longer than it was.

I took the stairs one at a time, laden with her in my arms, but she was a slight wisp of a thing, and easy to carry. "You're gonna be alright, babe. You're gonna be just fine. We're almost to our room now, okay?"

She nodded silently. At least here, in the stairwell made of iron and concrete, the sounds of the storm outside were muted, and the storm raged in the distance.

Here, we were alone.

I continued the ascent until we got to the top floor. Shifting her up on my shoulder, I opened the door to the landing, and gently slid her to her feet on the dark gray carpet that lined the hallways. She opened her eyes and looked around.

"Thank you. How will I ever repay you?"

I smirked and winked at her. "I'm sure we can come up with some ideas..."

Her eyes opened wide and her mouth dropped open, but I just chuckled.

"I'm only joking, honey."

I wouldn't take advantage of her. I might be a monster who'd killed people for revenge, but I would not take advantage of a girl. Even I had some morals. They were few and far between, but I had them.

"Come on," I said. "Your suite awaits." The carpet was worn thin with wear, but it was clean, and the hallway vacant, as I led her to our room. There were no sounds other than the pitter-patter of rain, and I wasn't sure if it was because we were too far away from it, or if the storm really was dying down. I moved her along with me and slid the card into the slot that opened the door to our room. The light above the handle blinked green.

When I pushed opened the door and led her into the dark, vacant room, her eyes grew fearful. I was, after all, a complete stranger, about to take her into a hotel room, and maybe it was at that point she realized this wasn't the smartest move a girl could make. "I'm not gonna hurt you, Gabriella," I said, intentionally making my voice lower and softer. "You're safe, babe. Let's get you in and dry, yeah?"

She nodded, following me, and the door clicked shut behind us. If she were any other girl, I'd be plotting my move now, how I'd seduce her into doing what I wanted, the quickest, mildly ethical way from point A (fully clothed) to point B (naked, fucking her). But right then, the only thought I had was how I'd get her dry, and how I'd keep her safe... from whatever made her scared. From whatever might keep us apart.

From me.

CHAPTER FOUR

*W*here were we? What had happened? I had a vague recollection of him pulling me into the hotel, with nothing else available but the open road and his bike, amidst the most terrifying thunderstorm I'd ever seen. And now... what the heck had I done? Who was this guy? I was soaked to the bone, my clothes clinging to me as I looked around the large, kinda cute, but definitely not fancy hotel room.

He walked around the room, and what he did next was a little weird. He opened the closet, scanned it, then shut it as if satisfied it was vacant. Next, he moved to the bathroom, flicked the light on, grabbed a stack of towels, and tucked them under his arm before he flicked the shower curtain open, and then shut that door and the light to the bathroom off. After that, he moved around the bed—oh, God, there was *only one bed*, and a couch—looked around the edges, at the table beside it, and the small desk in the corner. What the heck was he doing?

The storm seemed far in the distance now, only bright flicks of lightning outside the window fading every few minutes. And suddenly, I was exhausted. Wet, cold, a little frightened, and so, so tired.

"No boogeymen in the closets?" I teased, wrapping my arms around my soaking-wet body to warm myself. He'd sobered, not even a glint of humor in his eyes. He didn't respond.

I shivered, and I wasn't sure if it was because of the cold.

Who was this man? Something inside me screamed a warning, that he was not safe, he could not be trusted.

But he'd held me when I screamed. He'd carried me up the stairs so I wouldn't cut my feet. And even now, he was ensuring my safety.

Finally, satisfied that we were alone and our temporary home was safe, he sat on the edge of the bed. "Gabriella, come here, please."

Though he said please, there was command in his voice, and my body instinctively responded. My belly dipped, my heart sped up, and my mouth went dry.

What would he do?

I walked to him slowly, my eyes on him, taking him in as I made my way over. His hair was sopping wet, darker now, almost a medium brown as it hung across his forehead, nearly shading his dark brown eyes. His shirt clung to him, and through the transparent fabric I could see the outline of his chest, strong and muscular, and thick black tattoos that ran along the edges of his shoulders and slashed down at startling angles.

Scary. Dangerous.

Hot.

When I didn't come quickly enough, he lifted a stern brow and stared at me, his lips pursed. "I need to see if you're okay," he said. "You were fucking terrified out there."

"Yes," I whispered. It was embarrassing, now, how I'd lost my mind like that. But he didn't know what thunderstorms and dark closets did to me. How could he? He'd probably been raised by normal parents. Nice people. People who loved him.

"I'm fine, now," I said. "And I'm sorry."

He shook his head from side to side. "You were scared, babe. Fucking *terrified*. And there's a reason for that. You don't need to apologize." Ok, so if he was a serial killer or something, he was a sweet one. "C'mere," he repeated gruffly. When I was within arm's reach of him, he pulled me to sitting on one knee and tipped a finger under my chin.

Oh my God.

"You okay now? The truth, Gabriella." I looked out the window, and I knew that yes, I was okay now, just a little mortified because of how I'd behaved.

I looked down at the floor. "Yeah, I'm fine now. I always lose it during severe thunderstorms," I whispered, my voice shaky, but I needed to tell him. "It's the only thing I'm really afraid of, Dante. I can't help it. I've tried to overcome it, but somehow, I just...can't."

He held me against his chest, and as he wrapped his sturdy arms around me, I stopped shivering. He was strong, and he was warm, even though we were both still soaking wet. "It's okay," he soothed. "It's over now. Maybe someday you can tell me why you're so afraid of thunderstorms. But now that you're calm, we need to get you out of these wet clothes."

Foreboding pooled in my stomach. What was he going to do?

"Go take a hot shower. Leave your clothes to dry and take this." He released me and handed me a large white towel. "I know it's weird because you don't even know me, but I promise I won't touch you."

A little blip of disappointment shot through me.

I wanted him to touch me. My face must have fallen, because he laughed. "You look let down, babe," he said, his laugh as dark and seductive as melted chocolate. "Go take your shower, and maybe if you're a good girl, I'll give you another kiss."

He gently pushed me off his knee and gestured for me to go to the bathroom. I blinked, looking around the room. When I came out wearing nothing but a towel, what would he do?

"Go, Gabriella, before you catch cold," he said, his voice deepening now, and his eyes grew stern. I shivered. God, it was delicious when he commanded me like that. And right then, in that moment, having been kissed by a man I hardly knew, standing in the middle of a hotel room with the hottest guy I'd ever seen, I felt oddly brave.

"Or what, bossman? You gonna spank me again, like you did to get me to move? You think I forgot that?"

His eyes flared with something I couldn't decipher, a kind of heat that made my belly warm and my pussy clench, as his lips twitched and his voice dropped. "Yeah, baby," he said in a deep rumble. "You do what Daddy says, or that's exactly what I'll do. I'll take you over my knee, and believe me, you *won't* forget it."

Ho-ly *shit*.

I turned to the bathroom and scooted in, chased by his low, dark chuckle.

Over my knee.

You won't forget.

Daddy.

Oh my *gawd*.

I had no idea why I was so turned on but I wanted it, all of it—to be taken over his knee and spanked, and to hear himself say *daddy* all over again. It was nothing I'd ever experienced before but I needed it, like, *now*.

I looked around the little bathroom. It wasn't the fanciest

thing I'd ever seen, but there was a lock on the door, which I clicked into place, imagining him hearing it on the other side of the door and doing... what? Cracking his knuckles or something? Then I looked in more detail around the bathroom. Despite the fact that he'd removed a stack of towels, there were at least four or five more, and thank God for that because I had to do something with my wet clothes, and I wasn't exactly going to parade around in front of a man I hardly knew with nothing on.

Thankfully, I was small, and one of the towels would fit me well. But as I glanced around the bathroom I realized there were two robes on the back of the door. I tiptoed over, eyeing them suspiciously. There was something a little weird about there being robes, like this was some sort of B-level spa, but I sniffed them and was pleased to discover that they smelled clean, like mountain fresh something and a little bleach. I'd do anything for my own robe from home, but this would be better than prancing around in a towel.

I opened the shower, and found it sparkling clean (thank *God*), and on the shelf were brand new little bottles of shampoo, conditioner, and a lavender-scented body wash that would be really nice. It took me a minute to figure out how to turn the thing on, but when I did, hot, steaming water beckoned me to come in and wash away all my troubles, to distract me from the fact that Sexy Prince Charming sat on the other side of the door.

I stripped out of my soaking wet top, peeled my jeans off, and tossed everything in a heap on the counter of the bathroom, then stepped into the stream of deliciously hot water.

I lathered myself up, breathing in the delicious floral scent, scrubbing my body with a fluffy clean washcloth, then lathered my hair with some of the shampoo. I used dollar store toiletries at home these days, nothing like the organic stuff mom used to buy, but it served its purpose. Didn't really matter what my hair looked like or what I smelled like, when I'd only be spending my day at the restaurant, waitressing, cleaning, and whatever other tasks that needed doing.

But here... this night was magical. And yeah, this was no fancy place, but it was head and shoulders above anything else I'd experienced before. And as I washed, I started to fret a bit.

I was a mess, and Dante had rescued me. Did he think me some sort of needy little girl? Someone who couldn't handle herself, or act responsibly? I sighed, closing my eyes as the stream of water washed away my grime, my tears, and my bravado.

"Useless," my stepmother said.

"Stupid," my step sister called me.

"No one would ever want you," Elenora had said just the day before.

Oh, how I longed for the carefree days of my youth, when my mother would tell me I was her special girl, and that she was proud of me. And my father... I choked back a sob. He would always make me feel beautiful and cherished, and we would laugh at the silliness of the world around us, forgetting everything that troubled us.

I didn't know how long I stood there, but the water had grown a little tepid, and I suddenly realized how selfish I'd been. As I daydreamed in the heat of the shower, allowing myself momentary longing for what used to be, I'd taken up all the hot water. What about Dante? He was just as cold and wet as I was, and I was sure he needed to warm up too. As quickly as I could, I rinsed my hair and body, shut the shower off, and stepped out. I wrapped myself back up in that big, fluffy towel, ran my fingers through my hair, and snagged the smaller of the two robes, twisting it about me, and tying the knot at my side.

"Gabriella?" God, in that ten minutes I'd been in there,

I'd forgotten how deep his voice was, so much so that it startled me and I jumped a little.

"Y-yes? Coming out now!" I hollered, suddenly afraid to open the door. When I did, he was sitting at the desk and he'd... oh, *God*... stripped off his wet t-shirt and hung it up on the side of the desk, in front of the heating vent that blew warm air into the room.

"Hand me your clothes," he commanded, his back to me, and I allowed myself a moment to take in the glorious sight of his beautiful, tattooed, muscled back.

I wanted to run my tongue along the edges of his muscles and snake my fingers down his chest...

"Gabriella?"

Oh my God! I was out of my ever-loving mind.

"Yes, of course, just a minute," I said, turning back to the bathroom and snagging my bundle of clothes. "Here, you don't have to do that for me," I said, but he merely raised a heavy brow, pursed his lips, and waited. Silently, I handed him my clothes.

I jumped when he snapped them open one at a time, smoothing them out, and laying them across the bare area where warm air blew from vents. He snickered to himself. "These are so tiny," he said in his deep voice.

I didn't know how to respond, so I didn't.

"Ok, did you leave me any hot water in there?" he asked, and I felt a moment of chagrin before he turned to me, giving me a lopsided smile that made my belly turn to mush.

"Erm... well... sorry about that. It was so luxurious in there, just standing under the hot water. I could've stayed for hours, but then I remembered you needed a shower, too..." I trailed off.

His lopsided smile turned into a full-on grin. "Luxurious. You found this hotel's bathroom luxurious? Babe, I can practically see the floor through the carpet. Did they somehow miraculously make the bathroom fancier?"

"Well, no, but at home we just have a standing stall thing and my sisters are always pounding on the door for me to answer. And I only have cheap toiletries, so..."

"I see," he rumbled, without further comment. "Be back in a minute. Be a good girl while I'm gone, yeah?" I squirmed.

Oh, God, he was so sexy I wanted to die.

"Sure thing," I said, saluting him as I plopped on the bed and lifted the remote. "I'll just sit here and watch TV or something."

He snickered, shook his head, and went into the bathroom. As he was in there, I wondered if I should take advantage of the opportunity. Find out who he was, maybe. What did they do in the movies? I could maybe frisk his jeans for his wallet, or... something? But I realized two things pretty quickly. First, what exactly would the purpose be? And second... he was still wearing his jeans.

I flipped through the channels instead, and as I lay there, warm and dry, my eyes grew heavy. It seemed like only moments later the cranking of the shower woke me from my sleep.

I rubbed my hands over my eyes as the door to the shower opened and he stepped out, wearing, predictably, just a towel wrapped around his waist.

I couldn't tear my eyes away.

His broad, powerful shoulders filled the entire doorway. The defined muscles on his chest looked sinfully delicious, as did the thin, dark line of hair that ran down his trim waist, all the way to... Oh, my.

Yeah, I was staring.

"Were you asleep?" he inquired. "Don't let me disturb you. It's late, and you probably have to get back early in the morning. I do, too. Phone's probably blowing up already," he grumbled. "You take the bed. I'll take the couch."

"You can't do that, Dante," I protested. "You're ginormous, and I'm tiny. I should take the couch." I got up out of the bed and rummaged in the little closet until I found a blanket, then tossed it on the couch. "But yes, I am awfully tired, and as grateful as I am for everything you've done for me—honestly, you've been *amazing* through all this—I really should get some sleep. What time did they say they served breakfast again?"

But I stopped talking then because the humor had fled his face and he stood, still in his towel, glaring at me, his hands on his hips.

"You're not taking the couch. Get back on the bed." He jerked an angry thumb back at the double bed.

No way. *He was not gonna do this.*

"Thank you again for your kindness, but this is hogwash. You know you won't fit on that couch, and how exactly are you supposed to ride that bike of yours back to town with a crick in your neck and a sore back? Hmm?" I lifted my chin at him. "I'm taking the couch... end of story. Now stop trying to boss me around, and let me sleep, please."

I turned my back to him, hoping he'd see I meant what I said. He pulled the blanket up over my shoulder, but a second later I squealed, limbs flailing, as he lifted me up bodily and hauled me over to the bed.

"The hell you are," he growled.

"Put me down!" I pounded on his huge back but it was like a kitten batting a moth. He paid me no mind and merely whacked my ass, hard, and plopped me down.

My blood rushed in my veins and my body betrayed me, wanting *more. Harder.*

"Behave yourself, Gabriella. I can tell you're a good little girl, but you remember what I told you I'd do before you took your shower." He wagged a finger at me. Miraculously, his towel was still astride his hips, he hadn't lost it. I squirmed and glared at him, but it was no use. I was overpowered, and way, *way* turned on, my glare simply a facade for what I really felt.

"Listen, Dante," I said.

"No, Gabriella, you listen to me. I'm not going to hurt you. I'm not going to take advantage of you. But do you *really* think that a guy like me, who'd fucking carry you up the stairs so you wouldn't cut your foot on the glass, would let you sleep on the couch? Jesus. I'll sleep on the couch, you'll sleep on the bed, and I swear to God you talk back to me again, and you won't sit for a fucking week."

His beautiful brown eyes were narrowed on me, daring me to disobey, making me listen, and his voice, though calm, barely held the edge of control.

I don't know what happened, then. I don't know if it was the fear, or the really strange, weird, messed-up night, or the fact that I was mad at myself for being turned on by his caveman-like tendencies, but without even thinking about it, I picked up the pillow next to me and whipped it straight at his beautiful, furious face. It smacked the side of his head, and he reared back, then it slithered along his body and fell to the floor in a heap.

My heart leapt to my throat and a quiver ran through me, as I wondered what he'd say, or do. A long, tense filled moment passed and no words were spoken. But his eyes bore straight into me and a muscle twitched in his jaw.

"What'd I say?" he finally whispered, in a dangerously low voice, prowling closer to the bed. I scrambled to the other side. I wasn't afraid, really, more excited than anything, and I wanted to hide the fact that I was.

"You said not to talk back. I didn't talk back. I—I threw a pillow. That is technically not talking back. And fine! I'll sleep on the bed. That huge, monstrous, cavernous bed, all by myself, while you cramp yourself on that teeny, likely filthy, crumb-ridden little couch!"

He reached me then, and before I knew what was happening, he plunked me straight over his lap.

"Dante! Dante, don't you—ow!"

I yelped, more startled than in pain, as his huge hand slapped against my ass. Pain blossomed into heat, which wove its way through my core, and my clit zinged with need.

Another sharp spank landed. "God, you need a good, hard spanking," he said, giving me another good whack. I felt him beneath me, hard as a *rock*. He was turned on. Oh, *God*. So it wasn't just me.

He didn't even lift my robe, and I was ready to climax right over his knee.

"Stop it!" I said, scissoring my legs. I flailed a hand behind me, wishing he would know I both wanted him to stop and yet I didn't. I wanted him to make it hurt, to really sting.

Who was I? Had I gone insane?

"Dante, please!"

"Kick your legs again, you lose the robe."

"No!" I sputtered. "You wouldn't. You said you wouldn't take advantage of me."

"I fucking won't. But you're under my protection tonight whether we want this or not, Gabriella." He wasn't spanking me now, and he'd only given me a few good whacks, but my clit throbbed painfully, my full breasts pressed up against his nearly-bare knees, and beneath my belly, his erection made me hum with desire.

I wanted *so* much more than a spanking.

"Is this what you do to all the girls? All your girlfriends? You spank them into submission like that Christian whatever something guy in that movie?" I hadn't seen it, but my sisters raved about it, and I knew they found it hot.

"If they're rude and bratty? Fuck yeah," he said.

His hand smoothed over the thick bathrobe covering my ass, which stung despite the extra padding. "Ok! Ok, Dante, I'll be good," I said, and I didn't recognize my own voice. Filled with lust, it was husky and breathy, but he didn't seem to mind.

"You gonna behave yourself?" he asked, his large palm smoothing over my robe again and beneath my belly, his cock twitched. *God.*

"Yes," I whispered. "I honestly really do behave myself most of the time, you know. I don't break the rules. I don't smoke or drink, and I even pay out-of-state tax, like if I cross the border and buy something? It only happened once, but I made sure I looked it up and paid it. And if I ever—"

"Gabriella."

"And I won't give you a hard time. I just feel—guilty, is all. You've been so good to me and you don't even know me. I don't really know exactly what it is you need or want from me, but if you just want me to stay in this huge bed alone, then fine, I will—"

"*Gabriella.*"

Draped over his knee, still completely out of my mind with arousal, I sighed. "Yes?"

"Come here."

He lifted me up and placed me on his lap, then tapped my chin. "You need a hug?"

I nodded against his chest, oddly turned on even more by his tenderness than I had been by his spanking me, and that was saying something.

"Yeah," I whispered. "A hug would be nice." He pulled me tighter against him, and I closed my eyes, allowing him to comfort me. It was sweet. No one had held me like this in so, so very long that tears came to my eyes.

"God, this has been a long day, huh? Why are you so afraid of thunderstorms?"

Even though I was turned on and needed more than a hug, I felt... safe. So safe, which was ironic considering the fact that he'd just spanked me.

"She used to lock me in the closet when I didn't do what she told me to," I whispered.

His body tensed. "Who, baby?" The rumble of his voice showed me his protective instincts had kicked in again. "Your mom?"

I shook my head. "No. No, never my mom, definitely not. My stepmother. And one time, she locked me in the closet when I was little, and there was a terrible thunderstorm. I felt like I couldn't breathe, and I thought I was going to die. I screamed but she didn't come for me." A shudder wracked my body and I burrowed closer. "She'd left me, and gone to bed, and forgotten all about me. My imagination ran wild, and I was so afraid that the lightning was going to electrocute me, and I was young enough that I managed to convince myself that the thunder was the footsteps of a huge giant ready to come and eat me."

"Jesus," he hissed. "My father's an asshole, but even he can't top that."

"Yeah," I mumbled. "She isn't a very nice person."

"This the stepmother you work for now?" he asked.

I only nodded.

"She sounds like a total bitch," he gritted out.

"Well, she was good enough to hire me, though," I explained. "If she didn't, I'd have nowhere to go. No home. Nothing."

He didn't say anything for a while. "Well, I'm glad the thunderstorm's past," he finally said. "And it's not like you're the only one who gets scared of them. I just wanted to know why. And now I do. C'mon, let's get you to bed."

I didn't want to get to bed. I wanted him to kiss me. This was a night that would never be recreated, I knew that much. Even if he *was* the kind of guy I could be with, my stepmother would never allow it. I worked from dawn until dusk every day and I never had time for myself. If she saw something that would take me away from my work... something I liked... she'd end it.

She always had. Always would.

I'd considered finding a place out from underneath her thumb, but she'd been married to my father. She'd been his wife, and a sense of loyalty still tethered me to her.

Tonight, though. Tonight, was not going to happen again.

"Before I go to bed, may I thank you just one more time?" I whispered pleadingly. "Just once, Dante? Please?"

His eyes crinkled around the edges and his beautiful lips twitched. "The way you did before?"

"Yes."

He rumbled a laugh. "You can thank me all you want, honey."

And so I lifted my face to his, and when I did, just like it had before... magic happened.

Shocks of arousal spiraled through my body, and my ass, still hot from the spanking he'd given me, ground into his cock. He wove one huge, strong hand through my hair until he reached the base of my neck, and tugged my head back. The pain spiked along my scalp and he swallowed my moan with another kiss, his lips around mine in a secret lover's promise of so much more to come.

I squirmed on his lap, completely out of my mind with lust, when his hand left my hair and trailed down to a shoulder, slipping the robe off and revealing bare skin. His rough, calloused thumb traced its way over my shoulder, and I gasped with the shock of his skin on mine. I needed more. I wanted to feel him. I *had* to.

I let my legs part open and moved even closer to him, silently begging him to do more than kiss me. He heard my plea, and his hand snaked under the soft folds of the robe, gently caressing the swell of my breast. I felt his cock beneath me and his own moan mingled with mine as he slowly, tenderly, explored my breasts, weighing the fullness with his palm and gently kneading before his thumb grazed my hardened nipple.

"Oh, God. Don't stop. Please, please, don't stop," I begged. I needed more, so much more.

"The second you tell me to stop, we stop," he whispered in my ear. "But I won't stop until then. I want all of you, Gabriella. You're beautiful." His mouth went to my ear and he took the lobe in his mouth, gently biting down. I gasped then melted, as he continued to whisper, "So... fucking," a twitch of his fingers on my nipple. "*Beautiful.*"

My head fell back as he worked me over with his tongue and his mouth, and the next thing I knew, I was on my back on the bed, the robe falling open as he gently unfastened the tie at my waist.

"Dante, there's something you should know," I gasped, as his mouth went to my breast and he pulled a nipple in his warm, sensual mouth, his other hand going to my other breast and fondling gently.

"Mmm?" he asked, as desire zinged through every inch of me.

"I-I'm a virgin," I said, tossing my hand over my forehead and closing my eyes as the edge of his teeth grasped my sensitive bud. "I know, a woman my age, and that would be twenty-one, never having had sex in her life—it's awkward and maybe a little weird. But I just wanted you to know that... well, that I don't have any idea what I'm doing at *all.*"

He chuckled.

"You think being a virgin is a bad thing?" he asked. "God,

no. I think it's awesome. You're pure. Untouched. And I can bring you to places you've never been, yeah, baby."

"I-I don't. I—well," I stammered, my eyes closed. "Sounds good," I finished stupidly, and his full-on rumble of laughter made me cautiously peek one eye open.

"Alright, baby," he purred. "You took your spanking like a good girl. And God, that was so fucking hot having you over my lap like that."

"Hot? You thought it was hot? So it wasn't just me then. I thought I was weird, being turned on by being spanked like that, but I've never been spanked, so how would I know? You're just so strong and... and... sexy, and, God, I wish we had some alcohol or something."

"Gabriella?" he asked, his breath now at my breasts as he lapped at the valley between them and I whimpered.

"Yes?" I croaked.

"You talk too much, baby. Way too much. It's adorable, but right now, you be quiet for Daddy, yeah?"

Daddy? Oooooooh, yes.

"Mmmm," I said, needing to obey this man. "Mmmhmmm."

Yes, Daddy.

"That's a very good girl. I love that you're such a very good girl. Now I won't fuck you, not tonight, though I want you to know it's not because I wouldn't love every fucking minute. Yeah?"

I nodded, again not wanting to talk after he told me not to. "But let me pleasure you, baby. You've never had a man touch you like this?"

I shook my head from side to side. He shot me a lopsided grin that made my insides melt.

"You wanna talk, don't you?" he asked, his mouth just over the middle of my belly now. *Oh God,* he was going lower. What was he going to *do?*

I nodded my head wildly up and down.

"No talking, baby. No moving. You do what Daddy says or Daddy'll take that tie around your waist, tie your hands to the bedpost, and whip your pretty little ass with his belt. Yeah?"

Eeeeeeep. I felt my eyes widen, my thighs dampen with arousal and my pelvis literally twitched. He chuckled. "That's what I thought, baby. Now you stay right there. You keep your hands where I put them. The only thing you can say is, *Please, Daddy.* You got that?"

I nodded.

I felt like royalty, the way his gaze traveled appreciatively over my virgin skin.

"I'm gonna have my way with you now, Gabriella. But I promise I won't fuck you." He shook his head slowly from side to side, his lips quirking up at the edges, the warmth of his breath heating my skin. My pelvis rose, silently begging him to do whatever he was going to do that I was gonna love. I stared at him and realized I'd stopped breathing, watching his tongue slowly lap at the sensitive skin right around the tops of my thighs. "You taste delicious," he rasped against my bare skin. "And I haven't even gotten to the good part yet." I saw him shift, one of his hands dipping below where I could see, and I suspected then he'd taken his cock into his hand. Just the thought made me whimper with need.

The very edge of his tongue tickled my skin, heading lower and lower still. Without warning, he sank his teeth into the sensitive skin. I gasped and writhed. My hands reached for his hair and I buried my fingers in the thick, coarse tresses, tugging as he licked and teased and made his way to my clit. I needed more, I needed his mouth on me so damn bad.

Another lazy trail of his tongue along the edge of my belly had me near-frenzied with desire, and then ever so slowly, he dragged his tongue along my slit. My hips bucked and I moaned so loudly I felt as if the sound had been wrenched from me.

"Please! Dante. Oh, God, stop torturing me!" I gasped, and before I knew what I was doing, I yanked his hair.

And then suddenly, his teasing stopped.

He rose, fastening his towel around his waist. His jaw clenched and his eyes were aflame.

Uh. Oh....

I scrambled back on the bed.

"I wasn't supposed to do that, was I?" He stalked over to me, shaking his head from side to side.

"You, um, maybe told me to be quiet, right?" I whispered, still scrambling backward so that my back slammed against the headboard and I had nowhere to go, but he was still advancing on me, his powerful body tensed with a controlled anger that made my mouth grow dry.

"What'd I tell you I'd do if you moved?" he asked, reaching for my chin and holding me in place so that all I could do was stare into his eyes.

My heart hammered so crazily I was afraid it'd leap out of my chest. Oh, God!

"Um, you said if I—ohhhhh..." I lost my bravado as his hand tightened in my hair. "You said if I moved you'd tie me up and spank me with your belt." The last words came out in a squeak, as he held my hair in his hands and nodded. His mouth came to my ear then and he whispered to me, "Have you ever been spanked with a belt, little girl?"

I shook my head. "Nooooooo, and I'm not really, um, so sure that I—eeeee!"

He'd lifted me straight off the bed, and with a firm tug, removed the belt from my robe.

"Dante! Oh my God! What are you going to do? I don't really—oh my goodness!"

I was on my knees, my hands out in front of me, and he

was tying them together. His mouth came to my ear and he whispered in a low growl. "This is about you, baby. This is about your pleasure. But tonight, I'm in charge, and you'll learn what it means when you disobey me. Daddy's gonna whip your ass. But I promise you, baby. You'll like it."

"You keep your hands right here," he whispered in my ear. "I have reasons for wanting you to do what I say, Gabriella. You'll see that following my lead will make it that much better for you. I like knowing you'll do what I say. I like control..."

I nodded as the soft folds of the robe tie trailed over my wrists, and he cinched them tight. "Stay here," he said, all tenderness gone from his voice as he commanded me in place. "You stay *right there*."

Um, where was I going to go?

I craned my neck to look over my shoulder and gasped as he lifted his jeans. With a tug, his belt came loose and dangled in his hand. Tucking the buckle into his palm, he wound the belt over his hand until he left a strap dangling. I squirmed a bit but a slow shake of his head told me to stop.

Was it going to hurt badly? What had I done to deserve this?

Oh, yeah. I pulled his hair. And maybe I talked a little bit when he told me not to. Alrighty, then.

Standing behind me, he pointed to the bedframe and twirled his finger. "Face the headboard."

His low, raspy voice made my heart patter in my chest.

Trembling, I obeyed.

"Good girl," he said. "Daddy will take it easy on you. You're new to this, aren't you, baby?"

I could only nod, not sure if I was allowed to speak or not.

His voice deepened. "Grab the headboard."

It was my only warning. I anchored myself just in time, as seconds later I heard the whizz through the air before his belt snapped against my bare ass. I yelped. It hurt, but not badly, more like a zing followed by warmth. I swallowed hard and closed my eyes, as heat rose in my chest. My clit throbbed, my ass throbbed, my whole damn body was one big pulse.

He reared back and snapped the belt again, taking my breath away with the intensity. "When I tell you to stay put and behave, I mean it," he said, in a low, husky tone that made my belly quiver. "Do you understand?"

A whizz of his belt zinged through the air. "Yes, Daddy!"

Oh, God. Just saying the words had me shaking with want.

"You're new, honey, so tonight, let's call this a reminder. No need for your ass to be welted when you sit on the back of my bike."

A spike of delicious fear pulsed through me seconds before his belt snapped against my ass again. My eyes shut tight, I could only feel. My body begged to be touched, my mind on nothing more than how his mouth had teased and tortured me, as another smack of his belt landed. My ass was flaming hot, but somehow, the spanking made me more aroused than I ever thought possible. I couldn't take it, as one smack after another fell, and his hand trailed between my legs between smacks.

I needed more.

I heard the clink of his belt falling to the bed, and my mind was oddly above me, like I was floating, soaring.

"You stay right where you are," he growled. "Don't you dare fucking move. You let Daddy do what he wants to, now, and I promise you, it'll be worth it. Yeah?"

I could only nod my head feverishly. Um, yeah, I'd take it. And I'd already learned that disobeying him would get me spanked good and hard, which only made things worse because then I needed release more than anything.

"Good girl," he said, laying himself down on the bed

beneath me where I knelt, grasping the headboard, legs spread wide apart. Oh. My. God!

"You stay right there, baby," he whispered.

Again. Where was I gonna go?

He laid underneath me, as he propped himself up with pillows and grabbed my hips. I shook, knowing what he was going to do, knowing it was going to be unlike anything I'd ever experienced and that I couldn't stop him.

"That's a good girl," he crooned. "Such a good girl. Daddy whipped her ass, but she learned her lesson," he said, his raspy voice tickling the sensitive skin between my legs. I shook and whimpered, but he grasped my hot, stinging ass with his hands and anchored onto me, before he pulled my pussy right toward his mouth. He sucked my clit and my whole body jerked from the intensity.

"Dante!" I gasped, as he suckled my sensitive bud before swirling his tongue in delicious, sensuous circles.

"Good girl," he repeated, lazily taking me into his mouth, warm and sensual and soooo amazingly good. I couldn't take it. I writhed, near frenzied with the feel of his mouth on me, sweet, delectable torture. He pulled his mouth off my sex just long enough to remind me, "What do you say, Gabriella?"

"Please, Daddy!" I begged, tears pricking my eyes I was so desperate.

He grinned, nodded his head, and rasped, "You come for me, babe."

He brought me back to his mouth, gently suckling my clit before lapping again, and with the second brush of his tongue, I came. I shattered, every delicious spasm of pleasure shooting through me until I thought I'd burst with it, wave after wave taking over my body as I screamed his name, completely undone, totally at his mercy. I didn't even know who or where I was, as I felt nothing but blinding rapture, riding my climax while he drew every last drop of pleasure from my body.

Finally, I was falling to the bed, not even conscious of what I was doing as he tugged himself free, his cock hard, towel strewn over the bed. I wondered briefly if he would take me, but he didn't. My hands roamed his body in a sort of stupor and he let me stroke his rock-hard shaft right before his eyes rolled back and seconds after me, he came. "Sexiest fucking thing I ever saw," he moaned, as he snagged his towel and cleaned us both up. He grinned as he untied my hands. "Jesus, baby, you lit up like the Fourth of July. So responsive. So sweet."

I was suddenly so, so tired. I was dimly aware of him padding to the bathroom to grab a washcloth and another towel, cleaning up, then removing my robe. "Lift your arms, Gabriella." I obeyed, and he slipped his t-shirt over me. It was so soft and warm and smelled like him. "Get under the covers, Gabriella," he said. "You're exhausted, baby. You can't even keep your eyes open."

He was right. I was so wiped I couldn't even think straight as he pulled the covers up over me. "I'll wake you first thing in the morning," he promised.

"Thank you, Dante," I whispered, thanking him not just for the promise to wake me but for everything. It was my first time with a guy, and I would never, ever forget it. Basking in the afterglow of what we'd just shared, I closed my eyes and drifted off to sleep.

CHAPTER FIVE

The sweet girl was sleeping. What had I fucking done? She was a virgin, for Christ's sake, twenty-one years old to my thirty but no, I couldn't take it easy on her. Yeah, I enjoyed control in bed, alright, but this was crazy. I'd spanked her good with my belt, but she'd liked it. I knew she would, or I never would have done it. I'd watched her reaction when I threatened her, reading her, making sure it wasn't anger or fear but arousal that emanated from her.

Still. I always had to have the upper fucking hand. But, shit, that had been the sexiest thing I'd ever seen, and I was one crazy fuck. I'd had sex with so many women I'd lost count and had spanked a few. But never had I ever taken my belt to anyone. I liked dominating, knowing that the girl I was with would do what I said, but Gabriella—no one had ever come for me like that before. I smiled to myself at the recollection of her head thrown back, totally wild, as she'd climaxed so hard I'd thought she'd shout herself hoarse.

I stirred, my cock hard again at the memory. And then, after she'd come, no regrets. No embarrassment. She looked so beautiful with that sweet, satisfied smile on her face.

Completely drunk on being spanked and made to climax. I tucked the blanket around her shoulders and brushed a piece of hair off her face.

Everything she did was wide open. So happy, she made me smile. I shook my head. Where had she come from?

Tomorrow, I'd take her back home. I hated the idea of bringing her back to her cruel stepmother, though. Why couldn't she just leave her shitty family?

I almost smiled to myself, shaking my head sadly. The irony burned. She could say the very same thing about me.

Couldn't he just leave?

Yeah. No, life wasn't always that easy.

She rolled over and snuggled up close to me. I thought she was dead asleep, so it surprised me when she talked to me in a low, sleepy-drowsy voice. "Aren't you gonna get some sleep?" she whispered. All that, and she was thinking about me.

"Yeah," I said, snagging a blanket and heading for the couch. "You rest now, too."

I cramped myself up in the corner. It was really fucking small. I'd never be able to sleep here. Damn my macho ways. Still, I got as comfortable as I could, with my legs dangling over the edges of the couch, fluffing up a few pillows and tossing the spare blanket over my bare legs. I reached out a hand to where the clothes hung, and was pleased to feel they were nearly dry. I grabbed my boxers and slid them on, still warm from the heater, then turned over on my side, and almost fell onto the floor. Cursing, I righted myself.

"Oh for goodness sakes, come up in the bed with me," she said, her eyes still closed. "Promise I won't take advantage of you."

I chuckled. "No. Go to sleep."

"Suit yourself," she said, turning over and facing away from me. "But to be perfectly honest, I hear the rain outside and I'm having a hard time settling down myself, and would really appreciate just a little... warmth. You know?"

I hadn't even realized the rain was back. Poor girl. That did it.

I took my blanket and pillow and knelt on the bed, adjusting things. "No touching," I said. "I won't touch you, you don't touch me. Okay?"

"Deal," she said, smiling with her eyes closed. As I lay in the darkness, the warmth of her little body pressed up against mine through the blanket, I closed my eyes, ignoring the way my phone buzzed with messages and my stomach grumbled with hunger. She needed to rest, and so did I. I'd never given a fuck what girls thought about me, beyond them opening their legs and letting me have my way with them. Fuck, I liked it when they knew who I was and were scared to cross me. But Gabriella... no. She couldn't ever know.

Nothing else mattered now. Nothing else at all. For just one night.

I woke before the sun did. I'd slept soundly, but only for a short time, as always. Too much on my mind to ever rest for long.

I lay in bed with one eye open, feeling her all over me. Literally.

So much for not touching. She had her arm thrown across my chest, her knee hitched up on my belly. The feel of her soft, warm body pressed up against me made me hard all over again. I closed my eyes, allowing myself just a second of believing that this was real. That she was mine. That we had something good, and pure, and honest. That I wasn't a murderer, a man she would run from if she only knew.

I picked up my phone from the bedside table, and steeled

myself for the inevitable slew of missed calls and messages I'd have waiting.

I wasn't wrong.

Thirteen missed calls and twenty-five urgent messages waited for me. Frowning, I swiped through them. My dad didn't text or use a cell phone, but had his minions do it for him. The first string of texts was from my cousin Emilio, his father was second in command to mine.

You coming back? Your father's beside himself.

The next, an hour later. *You can't ignore him, Dante. You know he'll find you.*

He'd find me, all right, but it wouldn't be like it was when I was a kid and he'd punish me for running. No, not this time. I was bigger than he was now. I was stronger. And he couldn't bully me anymore.

Still, he'd fucking try.

He knows you left and he wants you home.

A few more said about the same, until finally the last one. *Your father wants you home.*

Of course he did.

I swiped and replied. *Needed some space. Didn't go far. I'm fine, be home for breakfast.*

And I would. Cold familiarity wound itself in my gut, and to appease the sickening feeling, I held Gabriella a little tighter, as if her innocence could ward off evil. Gently, I ran a hand down her back. My t-shirt was way too big on her, and hung off her shoulder, baring beautiful, pale, porcelain skin, and the faintest remnants of my bite marks. I smiled to myself and gently traced a finger over the mark. I liked the idea of her going about her day, fully clothed, still wearing my imprint upon her skin.

"You awake?" I asked her, shaking her gently. "It'll be sunrise soon, and I don't want you to get in trouble for being late to work."

She stirred and murmured something about sleep and coffee. My voice sharpened. "Gabriella."

She opened one eye and glanced up at me. "Mmm?"

"Time to get up, honey," I said, reaching down and giving her a playful smack on her bottom.

"Dante," she whispered, rolling over, the tip of her finger tracing the hair on my chest. "I don't want to go back. I want to stay here with you." The words hung in the air between us for a moment and I didn't know what to say, before she spoke again. "I know I can't. I know it's just a fantasy. Sometimes, it's fun to dream a little, though, isn't it? I don't even know you, and last night was super fun and everything and it wasn't just the sex." She flashed a radiant smile my way. "Though, you know, I could get used to that."

I jerked with laughter but held it in as she continued. "It's just that when I'm with you, I'm myself. And you're... gritty and badass that it makes me feel safe. Like when I'm scared, you'll protect me." She opened her eyes then and looked up at me. "And I don't just mean from thunderstorms."

I wanted to find who had hurt her, what they'd done, and I'd make sure they never touched her again. But, God, how could I? Taking her with me would put her in danger. Instead, I leaned in and kissed her forehead. "You can be yourself with me, Gabriella. And I will protect you—there's no question about that. But for now, we've got to get you home safe. Yeah?"

She nodded, and even though it killed me, I let her go. Sitting up, she rubbed the sleep out of her eyes, in that cute, adorable way of hers, before she ran a hand through her hair and gave me a wide-eyed look.

"It happened, didn't it?" she asked, shaking her head from side to side and then groaning as she grimaced. "Hay bale. I am wearing a hay bale, right?"

I tilted my head to the side, not even trying to hide my amusement. "Well... yeah. You could say that."

"Grrrrr." Her dainty fists balled up and she leapt out of bed, racing to the bathroom. I saw the light flick on and then heard her shriek.

"Oh my God, it's worse than ever!"

"You're fine, honey," I said through my laughter. "Now get dressed so I can get you something to eat before I take you home."

"Like this? You're gonna take me home looking like this? They'll think I'm the bride of Frankenstein."

"I don't give a fuck who they think you are," I growled. "Gotta get you home. Don't worry, I'll hide your hair under the helmet."

"Not helpful," she muttered from inside the bathroom. I shook my head. Sweet, unpredictable, and a little crazy.

"It's too early for breakfast. Sorry, princess, but we need to get you back. Don't worry, though, I'm sure they'll be serving something downstairs."

Her head poked out of the bathroom. Her hair was still wild but at least she'd flattened it down a bit. "That's fine. I really just want something small, like a donut or a muffin or something."

I nodded and pulled on my pants. "Ok, let's go." I went into the bathroom behind her and splashed water on my face while she towel-dried her hair, and as she stood there wearing nothing but my t-shirt and acting like it was the most natural thing in the world, I couldn't help it. I stalked over to her until her back was flush up against the counter, looped my fingers through the hair at the base of her neck, pulled her head back, and kissed her like I meant it.

Gabriella's hand splayed against my chest, a silent supplication not to stop. Her lips fit mine perfectly and my cock throbbed as her sweet, sexy moan vibrated through me.

Tightening my hold on her, I deepened the kiss, plunging my tongue into her mouth.

I finally pulled away, but I couldn't deny the truth.

She was meant for me.

"Breakfast," I rasped in her ear, my dick painfully hard.

"Breakfast," she breathed back.

"Now," I said. "Before I do something I regret."

"Mmmm," she mewled in protest. "What if I want you to do something you'll regret?"

I glowered down at her. "Don't test me little girl." On impulse, I swung her around and smacked her ass, a good crack that echoed in the bathroom, sending her scurrying away. She gasped and rubbed her ass but sent me a mischievous wink.

Not having anything to pack, it took us minutes to get our things together. I shot another quick text to Emilio, shoved my phone in my pocket, and took Gabriella by the hand.

"I want to tell you something, babe," I said, not caring if it was sappy or whatever. I had to be honest with her, right here, right now, where it was just the two of us. Exhaling roughly, I sat down on a chair and perched her on my knee. "I don't know what'll happen after today, but I want you to know that I enjoyed the hell out of myself last night. That... I'm glad I found you. That I think you're funny and brave and sexy as fuck. You remember that, yeah?"

Her eyes watered a bit but she just nodded before she leaned in and whispered in my ear. "Yes, Daddy. And thank you."

Jesus. My chest clenched, something possessive and proud taking hold.

I pulled her to me in a quick embrace, then released her, took her hand, and opened the door to usher her out.

As we walked down the corridor and turned the corner, I realized we weren't alone. One alcove that was vacant the night before no longer was. And I knew that in the parking lot were at least two more guys lurking about. Emilio was likely on the premises as well. Anger swirled in my stomach as Gabriella walked along beside me, oblivious to the fact that we'd been found, and we were being watched. Stalked.

Sick bastards. I fucking hated them.

I pulled out my phone and texted Emilio.

Get your fucking henchmen out of here. You found me, ok? Now leave me the fuck alone. I'm safe. Just needed fucking space.

I hit send and strode down the hallway with Gabriella's hand clasped tightly in mine, and a moment later, I felt them dissipate. I saw the hulking shadow of one guy leave the ice machine, and I knew Emilio was giving them the order to leave. They would pretend they were there for my safety, my protection, in case I'd been compromised in some way, but that was fucking bullshit. They were there to spy on me. Plain and simple.

"Can we still grab a bite to eat before we go?" Gabriella asked, still completely unaware of what was happening. My stomach pitched with the knowledge that this was why I had to bring her back.

I wanted her to keep that purity. That innocence. She didn't need to be tainted by evil.

"Sure thing, honey," I said. "Wouldn't want my girl to go home on an empty stomach."

"Nope," she said with a grin. "And I'm kinda *starving*."

I'd get her food even if I had to shake the little front desk guy by the front of his shirt and make him flip a fucking omelet himself.

"What do you want, babe?"

"A chocolate donut or a blueberry muffin, and coffee with cream, no sugar."

My lips quirked up in a smile.

We made our way downstairs, and I told her to wait for

me by the couches in the lobby while I spoke to the front desk clerk. "We need to check out," I said. Same kid as the night before. "I know it's early, but is there any chance you can get my girl something to eat now?" I peeled a crisp note from my wallet and slid it across the counter to him. He blinked at it, snatched it up, then nodded his head eagerly. "Yes, of course," he said. "Right away, sir! What would she like?"

"You got a chocolate donut or a blueberry muffin? And two cups of coffee, please. Mine dark, hers with cream."

He came back a short while later with food in a paper bag and two to-go cups.

"Thanks," I said, bringing her the things. "Check us out of room 342, please."

He nodded. "Done, sir."

I sat her down in the lobby to sip her coffee and eat her donut. "This is really yummy," she said. "I don't eat donuts much, but when I do I want them to be like this, fluffy and sweet and really chocolatey. You?" She licked the icing off her finger, her large green eyes watching me as I sipped my coffee.

I shrugged a shoulder. "Not a donut person," I muttered. "I like bacon and eggs."

She giggled and took another bite, speaking around the food in her mouth. "Spoken like a true caveman." I reached over, and brushed a crumb off her lip with the pad of my thumb.

"Damn right. Now finish that up so I can get you home." Her face fell, but she nodded, then gave me one final look through her long, long lashes.

"Yes, Daddy," she whispered. I smiled, a sort of sadness twisting in my gut. How could I let her go? We could never be together. It wouldn't be right. But I still couldn't bear the thought of never seeing her again.

"You're a good girl, Gabriella," I said in a low voice so only she could hear, taking a moment to tuck a piece of hair behind her ear. It seemed she always had a wild piece of hair escaping, and I loved that she did because it gave me an excuse to touch her in a way that was chaste, innocent, and tender. Her eyes met mine and as I held her gaze, I knew as well as she did that our time together was quickly dwindling. That after the sun rose, our magical night would be over. I bit back a low, angry growl of frustration.

What we had together was so much more than a one night stand, but this was not meant to be.

"Finish up," I said.

Her gaze cast down to her donut and she nodded.

"I'm ready," she whispered. "Let's go."

Beautiful, brave girl.

I took my keys out of my pocket, and held her hand as we walked.

I looked to where I'd parked my bike, and realized it was gone.

My fingers curled into fists as the cool morning air rose, my anger stoked by what I knew was a sign. There, a few rows behind where I'd left it, sat my bike. Fortunately, Gabriella didn't notice.

"Isn't it so nice how in the morning before the sun rises, it's a bit cool here? I mean, the second the sun does rise, it's hot as you-know-what and I could fry an egg on the sidewalk, but it's like the morning here defies the heat of the day. You know?"

No, I didn't know, but I did fucking love hearing her ramble.

"Yeah?" I said, scanning the narrow parking lot, wondering who was still hanging around. I could see it now, my father sitting at his desk in the darkness in his signature suit, hands folded as he ordered me found. "Unsettle him," he'd say. "Let him know we were there, but don't hurt him."

Fucking sick bastard. I was his son.

As if I could do anything but return?

I wordlessly took her small purse and held the bike so she could climb on first. She chattered incessantly about the climates of the south that were hot all the time and not inter-mittently like the places that had mountains or whatever the fuck, and I nodded and pretended to give a shit. Because the truth was, it didn't matter what she was talking about. I could listen to her talk all fucking day.

"But the little plant? It *died*, Dante. Just died. I'd tried to nurture it back to health with my own hand but I simply couldn't and it was an utter travesty." She sighed. "I buried it when it died, I was so sad about it, in a little plot in a garden outside the restaurant where my stepmother never went. If she'd found my plant she'd probably have punished me for doing something that took me away from my work."

The bitch.

"Yeah, baby?" I said, trying to placate her as I scoped out our surroundings to make sure no one else was lurking in the shadows. If anyone saw her, there'd be fucking hell to pay.

Once the coast was clear, I hitched a leg up and joined her on the bike, my gut soaring when her hands wrapped around me from behind. She felt so perfect there, on the back of my bike, holding onto me with complete and utter trust.

"Well, you know, miracles do happen, though."

Like fuck they did.

"And that little plant that I buried in a plot because it died? It came back to life. It grew in the spring. I had the perfect little spot with the sun and rain and I don't even know what else, but it grew. And it lasted for a very long time before a rabbit ate it."

I stifled a snicker as I kicked up the engine and pulled

onto the road, the faintest glow of the sun rising in the distance.

"A rabbit?"

"Yes," she said. "In my mind I imagined it was a mother rabbit fending for her babies and bringing them sustenance, and then I was okay with the second death of my plant. It was better it died with dignity and honor rather than because of malice or spite."

Were we still talking about plants?

Suddenly her little story meant a bit more to me and I paid closer attention.

"I'd agree with that, Gabriella. Yeah."

She was quiet then, and I sort of missed her talking. But I knew, already, even though I'd only known her for such a short time, that she was thinking.

"You're this big, tough guy," she said, breaking the silence. "And I know that if something bad happened you'd, you know, use your fists to defend me."

I smirked.

Fucking adorable.

"Yeah, honey, if I had to. Sure I would."

"Have you ever been in a fight?" she asked.

God, if she only knew. Did the sun rise in the east and set in the west? I was the son of the Mafia Lord of Vegas. Fuck yeah I'd been in fights. I'd defended the honor of the family with my own two fists, with cold metal, with certain death. I'd started them on purpose, too, because I needed an excuse to pound the shit out of someone.

"Yeah, unfortunately, I have," I said.

"Unfortunately?" she asked. "Why do you say that? Were they terrible?"

I frowned. "I don't like violence," I admitted, which was an ironic fact I had never actually said out loud until then. I was raised with violence, brutality my milk, weaned on blood-shed and power. But still... I hated it.

"Yeah," she said, her voice traveling in the wind. It was a thankfully quiet morning, so despite the fact that she had to raise her voice to be heard above the roar of the engine, I could hear her clearly. "I hate that for you, Dante. I'm sorry that you hate violence and have experienced it. I wish you never had to fight." She paused. "Though if I have to be honest, it's sorta cool pretending that you were fighting for me. Like one of those knights, you know, defending his lady's honor. Wow. That is like a majorly hot fantasy." She giggled. "Maybe it's the tattoos."

"Maybe," I mused. "And fuck yeah I'd defend you, baby. No matter what it took." The road gave way to more build-ings, more cars, and a busy intersection on the outskirts of where I needed to be. We both knew this was it, the moment where we would say goodbye and that likely would be the end. "Where am I taking you?" I grumbled, more harshly than I'd planned.

"Do you know where Five Corners is?" she replied, burying her face into my shoulder and tightening her grip around me.

I nodded. Yeah, I knew where it was. In the most anony-mous, busiest part of town, where she'd melt into the crowd and I'd never find her again.

I pulled to a stop next to the curb, in front of a bench, surrounded by people, hoping no one would see us, needing to bid her goodbye before they did.

"I wish I could give you my number," she whispered. "But maybe that's not a good idea."

My throat tightened as I held the bike steady while she got off, and then climbed off myself. I kissed her forehead fiercely and whispered in her ear. "I do know. And I can't tell you how much I wish I didn't."

She closed her eyes when my lips met her forehead, and it broke my heart to see a tear seep from beneath her closed lids. I'd give her anything, fucking *anything* to make her smile. She opened her eyes and smiled bravely at me, and I knew then I'd done something right in my life that someone so good, so pure, and so innocent would smile at me like that.

"Something tells me this isn't the end," she said, as tears streamed down her face unchecked and she shook her head from side to side. "Last night was so special, Dante... and I'll never forget it as long as I live." Her voice broke and she leaned in, placing her hand on my shoulder and whispering in my ear. "You think you're not a good man. But you're the very best there is. I don't know much, Dante, but I know this. I just do. It's in my gut. And I have good feelings about things like that."

I'd take it. I closed my eyes and buried my face in her soft, fragrant hair and swallowed the emotions that choked me, holding onto the one good thing that had ever let me close.

I held her tightly, and she gasped in surprise as I snaked my hand to the base of her neck, gripped her firmly, and brought her mouth to mine. I kissed her goodbye then, in a way that she would never forget. She came up on her toes and held onto my shoulders and kissed me back... in a way that *I* would never forget.

On impulse, I changed my mind.

"Tomorrow," I said. "Meet me here tomorrow at midnight. Can you do that?"

"Midnight," she repeated.

"Midnight, baby. Right here, by the water fountain with the pink lights on it."

"I'll be here," she breathed, her eyes alight, kissing the tips of her fingers and waving them at me. And then she was gone. She'd melted into the crowd as if she were one of them, but she wasn't. Not Gabriella.

I watched her go and allowed myself a moment to compose myself.

I had everything I wanted. The biggest mansion. The most expensive cars. A bank account that rivaled the leaders of small countries. A private jet that would take me anywhere I wanted. And it all paled in comparison to the one thing I really wanted.

Gabriella.

I'd wait for her, until tomorrow, at the stroke of midnight.

I watched her until she disappeared from sight, and then I got back on my bike, started the engine and went to where I knew he was waiting for me.

"*N*ot gonna tell me her name?" my father said, and I shook my head. When I was younger, I knew this was the point where I'd bear the wrath of his fury for my disobedience. I'd been bigger and stronger than him for a while now. Didn't mean my stomach didn't still clench in conditioned fear when his voice got that tone, though.

He nodded. "Alright, then. You're my son. You're entitled to a little privacy once in a while."

Fucking bullshit. I knew he was lying, but I wouldn't argue.

"You do know what this means, though, don't you? You found a girl you want to hide. Look at the position you've put me in, son."

My hands clenched in fists as I looked beyond him, at the gleaming framed print on the wall, not wanting to look at him, not able to meet his eyes.

"Very well," he said. "Your mother has an idea."

My mother? I looked back at him. "Yeah?"

He nodded. "You need to marry a wealthy girl, and if we

find those motivated by wealth then we find those less likely to have..." he waved a hand in the air. "Moral hang-ups about who you are and what you do. So at the end of the week, we'll have a masquerade ball. We'll invite the daughters of our contacts, the rich and powerful with daughters who would benefit from joining our family. You will meet them, and you will choose a wife." He paused. "It will be an honor for them to marry into the family."

"You want to have a party," I bit out. "And line them up so I can pick one out like my favorite flavor of ice cream." The insanity of his plan infuriated me. What the actual fuck was he thinking?

"You make it sound so cheap."

"It is cheap!"

"Enough!" he roared. I stiffened and frowned but said no more.

"This is business. People who say they marry for anything other than money or stature lie, Dante. They *lie*. I've been around long enough to know this."

What?

I looked at him in genuine confusion. "You married Mom for money or stature?"

His eyes met mine across the room, cold and brutal. "Of course I did," he spat out. "My father was Donatello Villanova, the most powerful man in all of Venice, and you think I could let my family bloodline be weakened? I married your mother because she was the heiress to Crowater Enterprises, and our ties strengthened both of our families." He looked away then and shrugged a shoulder. "She's a good woman, and we've grown to care for each other. This, you know."

I did. Didn't mean it didn't make my stomach twist with nausea.

I thought about Gabriella and what my dad would do to

her if she was ever in his presence, and I knew I had to do what he wanted me to. Letting him marry me off for the good of the family was the only choice I could make.

"Fine. Do it," I muttered. "Now." I got to my feet and his eyes flared with anger at the command I'd given him but I didn't give a fuck.

I shoved open the door to his office and went to leave. "And the next time I want some time alone, I'd appreciate you leaving your fucking henchmen at home."

"Dante!" His chair knocked back as he got to his feet, his old rage surfacing.

I turned and looked at him, pointing a finger his way. "Do you want me to be a leader in this family?"

"Of course," he spat. "But you'll remember your place."

As if I could forget. I turned on my heel and left, ignoring his demand for me to come back. "You want me to lead?" I called over my shoulder. "Then let me fucking lead."

CHAPTER SIX

$\mathcal{I}$t was easy to be nobody in Vegas. There were too many other people doing their own thing, drawing attention to themselves, noisy people who thankfully gave me the anonymity I craved right about now. The sun had begun to rise, but it didn't matter. Not here... in the city that never slept.

I easily melded into the crowd wiping away at the tears that simply would not stop.

Enough, Gabriella, I chided myself. *You have so many things to be grateful for. You did a careless, reckless thing, and you can't focus on that now.*

If she finds out, she'll hurt him.

The last thought came to me unbidden and I focused on that as a little thread of fear wove itself through my thoughts. I knew it was true. Agatha was overtly nice to me in front of others, but she thrived on my loneliness. If she thought for a minute that I'd found someone who made me happy...

Was she that evil? Was she really that self-centered?

For years, I'd told myself that my stepmother treated me the way she did because she grieved the loss of my father.

He'd loved her, and I guess she'd loved him back. She'd mourned his loss like any good widow would have, at least at first. She'd worn black, and dabbed at her eyes when people offered their sympathies, but the very week after we'd buried him, she'd had a new boyfriend.

She'd be waking up now. I glanced at the time on a large clock that hung in the marketplace, knowing my phone was still dead and needed a charge.

I opened the back door to La Bistro and clicked it shut behind me, then glanced around. Was she lurking somewhere, ready to ask me about my night? I wouldn't tell her. No, I would not, not for anything. But fortunately, she was nowhere to be seen. She never really was a morning person.

I filled and prepared the massive stainless-steel coffee pots and hit the red switches to brew the various blends, then made sure the carafes were filled with cold coffee cream, and all the sweeteners were in place. Shortly, the rest of the wait staff and cooks would arrive, and Manuel would lug the big pots out for me. For now, I had work to do.

As I did inventory on the breakfast sausage and eggs, I tied a bandana around my hair to keep it out of the food. I jotted down what we had, and what we needed, and as I bent over to peer at everything on the lower shelf, I felt the residual sting along my skin.

And I remembered how he stood, his belt in hand, commanding me to hold onto the headboard and not move. My heart raced.

Oh, God.

As I filled the pitchers with juice and put out the trays of little juice cups, I recalled the way he'd grabbed my hair and pulled my head back, unapologetic and commanding, taking without asking.

Dante.

God, Dante.

He was a man who would not cower in the face of fear.

He was fierce and strong, and protective.

As I snapped clean, white cloths onto the tables by the buffet line, and smoothed them down, I remembered what it felt like to lie naked under the blanket, having climaxed at his touch, the memory of his mouth on me still vivid and delicious. I jumped as I realized someone had arrived and was talking to me and I hadn't even noticed.

It was just Manuel, one of our staff.

"Morning, Gabriella," he said. "Your stepmother was looking for you. Have you seen her yet?"

"Um, no. When was she looking for me?"

"Last night. She tried calling your cell phone and couldn't get in touch. She was angry that she hadn't heard from her daughters. Seemed they weren't able to be reached either." He gave me a sad smile. "Eh, she'll be here soon enough, but don't worry. You know how we get busy on Wednesdays. She won't have time to nag." Manuel was an older, middle-aged man with dark hair and skin. He knew how to handle Agatha, and it was mostly by just smiling and nodding and ignoring her rants.

Maybe I needed to adopt his methods.

"Thanks. I went to a concert with Violet and Elenora, but they needed my seat and ended up ousting me, so I... came home myself." No need to tell him everything,

He paused, leaning the large pots against a table, "They left you?" he asked, his dark brown eyes angry beneath furrowed brows.

I nodded. "Yeah. But it worked out fine. Don't worry."

He shook his head from side to side. "They treat you so badly, Gabriella," he huffed, but I put up a hand to stop him.

If they hadn't left me like that, I never would have had the night I had. I closed my eyes briefly, suddenly overcome with emotion. "Believe me when I tell you it was fine." My voice shook a little. "That *I'm* fine. Okay?"

He gave me a long look, before returning to his work. "Alright, if you say so," he said. "But do me a favor, will you? No more concerts with them. You're tired at night because you work early morning hours. Got it?"

I smiled at him. "Okay." He was a good guy.

The atmosphere in the restaurant changed then, the second her heels clicked on the floor in the kitchen. "Morning!" my stepmother trilled, her voice holding a thread of control, the fake friendliness making me shiver. She was ruthless and mean, and only pretended to be kind to her staff for show.

"Morning, Agatha," I said brightly. "I heard you were looking for me last night?"

Better to confront her in a public place.

"Yes," she said, the smile fading from her face. She looked as if she were about to step on a runway, as usual. Her jet-black hair was twisted into a severe knot at the base of her head, her dark red lipstick and black mascara making her complexion appear pale white. She wore black stilettos and a skin-tight, olive-green sheath dress, emphasizing her fit figure. Her lips thinned as she eyed me.

"You didn't come to dinner, and I was worried about you, Gabriella," she said, her eyes flitting over to where Manuel was taking chairs down and setting them up.

"Well, you know the girls and I went to a concert," I said. "Turned out they needed my seat in the car after all, so I opted to—" I paused, almost saying "come home," but it would've been a lie and I didn't like lying. "Opted to give up my seat. I had a bit of a mishap with my phone dying, but I made it home, as you can see." I forced a smile. "Did the girls enjoy themselves?"

Her eyes narrowed on me. She knew I was hiding something, but I wouldn't let her pry. I turned my back to her and continued preparing breakfast. Customers would arrive in an hour, and our early morning breakfast buffet was popular for businessmen and women traveling, or the late-night people who'd pulled all-nighters at the casinos.

"Oh, Agatha? Did you order more juice? We're much lower than usual, because of the school outing that cleaned us out last week."

"Done," she said, as her phone rang and she took it out of her pocket tentatively, her long, sharp red nails clicking on the screen as she answered.

"Oh, hello," she purred, her eyes lighting up as she turned her back to me. Had to be a man, I reasoned. "Oh, yes. I would love to meet you for lunch today. But of course," she said, giggling her fake laugh that set my nerves on edge. "Please do. That would be delightful." Her voice dropped and her eyes scanned the restaurant. "Me, too, sweetheart. Me, too."

I shivered. What could my father have ever seen in this woman? My mother had been a good woman, gentle-hearted and loyal, and though she'd had no money growing up, she was never bitter. She'd taught me to be kind to people, to treat people the way I wished to be treated, to look at the bright side of things and be grateful. *Always something to be thankful for, Gabriella,* she'd say. Her wholesome beauty was in such sharp contrast to Agatha's that it boggled the mind.

"Gabriella, have you seen your sisters?" Agatha asked as she paraded about the dining room, straightening out a stack of napkins and flicking pieces of imaginary dust off the pristine tablecloths.

"Not since last night."

She didn't reply, merely turned the juice pitchers so they were all facing the same way, and shrugged a shoulder. "I suppose they were having too much fun," she said with a snicker. "Now, this evening, I won't be here," she informed me. "I'll be taking the girls shopping. So I expect you to do the closing circuit and ensure that everything is prepared for the weekend." She stepped over to me and leaned in to speak to me in my ear. "And there's no need for you to be making snarky public comments about my daughters' behavior. Do you understand me?" She reached a hand to my wrist and squeezed, so sharply I gasped.

"What are you talking about?" I asked, but we had no time to discuss it, as the wait staff and chefs had begun to arrive.

"Gabriella, order more paper goods," Agatha ordered, waving her hand at me while I trailed behind her with a notebook, taking notes. "Don't skimp on cost, like you did last time."

"Well, the last time I ordered, you told me to keep it under a hundred dollars, so I—"

"Do not contradict me," she snapped. "As I mentioned, your sisters will be busy this evening, so I want you to be sure you have proper wait staff in place," she said. Elenora and Violet were the ones who supposedly oversaw the evening shifts, but it was little more than a ruse. I oversaw the evening service as well as the morning crew, and Elenora and Violet did their own thing.

"Yes, certainly," I replied. She paused and pursed her lips, as the door to the restaurant opened and in walked Violet. Her hair was disheveled and she wore a tight-fitting red dress that dipped in the front, showing her ample cleavage. Her hair, dyed a vibrant red, clashed oddly with the color of her dress, but she didn't seem to care. She stepped into the restaurant holding her head high and when she saw me, she looked away guiltily.

"Violet," Agatha greeted, giving her a curt nod. "Nice of you to join us."

Violet rolled her eyes. "Oh, give it a rest, mother," she sighed, as she click-clacked her way over to us. "So I went out last night and didn't come home. I'm nineteen years old and an adult now, so you have no right to give me shit about it." Agatha's eyes narrowed on her.

"Old enough to not come home but still has mama pay her cell phone bill?" Agatha asked while she folded her arms across her chest.

"I don't need you to pay my cell phone bill, but if it's part of my salary then you have no business trying to make me feel guilty about it," Violet snapped. She had a point. However, they were causing a scene, as usual, and I needed to step in.

"Breakfast is underway, ladies," I said, trying to escort them back to at least the kitchen area of the restaurant. I couldn't sit down and eat myself, as I had far too much to do, but they often ate breakfast before the onslaught of customers.

"I'll have some," came a voice from the back entrance, as Elenora waved her hand at me, the back door jangling closed behind her. She wore a tight-fitting dress similar to her sister's, but as Elenora had more assets to fill it, the effect was something quite different. She was far shorter and curvier, with a full bust she accentuated as best she could. Her mousy brown hair hung about her in wild waves, and her brown eyes still bore the signs of smudged evening makeup. "I'm famished."

"Cinnamon roll French toast is loaded with calories, Elenora," Agatha chided, ever the food critic reminding her daughters to keep their girlish figures. And thus began the early-morning spat with daughter number two.

Thankful they could preoccupy themselves a bit with arguing, I made my way back to the front of the restaurant and opened the door. I breathed a sigh of relief when I opened the door and found my friend, Ruby Kitteridge, in her signature Hawaiian shirt. Ruby was a plump, kind-hearted older woman who lived nearby. She was independently wealthy, having lost her millionaire husband to cancer just the year before. A restaurant regular, she was a good friend.

"Good morning, Gabriella," she said, opening her arms for a quick hug. I had to stoop to put my arms around her. "Looks like your sisters are at it again with the Wicked Witch of the West, eh?" she whispered, giving me a wink. Her white hair was cut short, but she managed to tuck a stray lock behind her ear as she grinned at me. She wore large pearl earrings and a matching necklace, and if I knew her, they were not only real but worth more than my entire year's salary.

"Hush, Ruby," I said. "Let's get you seated." She took my arm and walked with me to the corner booth that she always occupied. "But yes, they're busy doing the usual."

Violet, Elenora, and Agatha were known for their spats. I mostly ignored them and stayed out of the fray, if I gave them the chance to focus on me, I typically became victim of their venomous insults.

"Hot tea, four sugars, double tea bag?" I asked her. Ruby liked her tea fixed just right, and I knew her usual.

"That's a dear," she said. "And since it's Wednesday, be a good girl and get me some French toast right off the griddle, won't you? You know how I feel about it getting all soggy in the buffet."

I smiled at her as she sidled up to her table.

"Of course. Just a minute," I said.

I tucked my notebook into my apron and made my way to the kitchen, taking a clean glass plate from the serving line and heading toward the grill.

"Manuel, an order of fresh French toast, extra butter, and heated syrup, please," I said, sliding the plate up to the serving line. He saluted me, when the voices of my sisters and stepmother reached me.

"How do you know?" Violet asked. "And has everyone been invited, or only a select few?"

"Private invitation," Elenora breathed. "But Vinny got us an invite. How many do you think will be there?"

I never paid any mind to the social gatherings and galas they attended. Even if I was interested, I had no time for such things. For some reason, though, what Agatha said next held my attention.

"Rumor has it, the king is trying to find his son a suitable match," she said. "And girls, if this is true, you absolutely must attend. There is no question how important this ball will be for your futures. If one of you marries into the family, the other will be set for life."

The girls squealed and clapped their hands.

The family? The king? Set for life? What were they talking about?

Shaking my head, I took the plate Manuel handed me and headed back out to the dining room.

Ruby grinned at me, and took her plate, before slathering it with butter and dousing it with syrup.

"You look different today, Gabriella," she said, tilting her head to the side.

Oh, how I wanted to sit and tell her everything, all about the magical night I'd had.

Well, maybe not *everything*.

I sat down at a chair next to her and smiled. "I had an amazing night, Ruby," I gushed. "I met this man...." My voice trailed off as she grinned at me.

"I knew it," she whispered with a little girlish squeal. "What was his name?"

"His name was Dante," I whispered, and my eyes fell on

the phone in front of her, still open to the morning headlines. "*Villanova family throws large masquerade ball for the elite.*"

The Villanovas... who were they again?

"Gabriella!" Agatha's screech had me leaping to my feet as she glared across the restaurant at me, her tone so harsh Ruby shook her head in indignation.

"That woman needs to get herself a goddamned hobby, one that doesn't involve telling you what to do," she grumbled under her breath, before turning toward my stepmother with a fake smile plastered on her face. "She was answering some questions I had for her."

"I'll be right back with the rest of your tea, Mrs. Kitteridge," I said. Agatha narrowed her eyes at me, and when I went to the backroom, Violet and Elenora were in a near frenzy.

"I have no idea what I'll wear," Elenora said. "The dress I wore to the Markhams' charity ball last year is way too small."

Violet gave her a sardonic grin. "You could just diet, you know, and then fit into it," she said. "Don't you think that's an option?"

I gave Elenora a sympathetic look, trying to silently tell her to ignore her sister, but it was no use. Elenora's temper had already flared.

"Maybe *you* can go on a diet," she spat at Violet. "I noticed you've gone up a size in your jeans, and when you asked Robbie to pick you up at the concert last night, the poor guy practically burst a blood vessel just scooting you up onto his shoulders."

"You bitch!" Violet screamed, picking up a nearby glass of water and tossing it toward Elenora, who ducked just in time... allowing the full force of the cold liquid to land on Agatha, who'd been standing just behind her.

My step sisters and I gasped in response, but Agatha just

swiped a stack of napkins, dried her face off, and glared at the girls.

"What. Are. You. *Doing*?" she roared, getting the attention of several employees nearby. "I told you *not* to fight in my restaurant."

"You called me, Agatha?" I asked, numb to the arguments of the girls and oblivious to any tone from Agatha.

"You two will go with me," Agatha said, shoving me out of the way. "Doesn't matter that only the elite will be there. We were elite once and we are still, if only the Villanovas would acknowledge that. After all, I was a princess, once..." Agatha's voice trailed off.

A *princess*? What on earth was she talking about? That was the most ridiculous thing I'd ever heard.

"Who is allowed to go to this?" I asked, earning me three shocked looks.

"Go to what?" Agatha asked with a sneer.

"This dance," I said.

"Were we talking to you?" Elenora snapped, her lip curling in disgust. I felt my stomach twist in anger.

"No," I said. "You weren't. But I heard you saying something that interested me, and I wished for more information. Is there something wrong with that?" The next second I was jerked backward, Agatha's hand wrapped around my hair.

"You do not speak to my daughter that way," she said, shoving me away. "Go see if the food needs refilling, and then come back here. We have work that needs to be done." She put her arms around the shoulders of both of her girls, and marched them in the direction of the office.

Sorrow rose inside of me and my thoughts went to Dante. He'd never allow anyone to treat me this way. Why did she hate me so? I reminded her of the husband she lost, maybe, I reasoned. There could be no other reason any one person would hate another so very much.

I wished for the millionth time that I could leave. I didn't care where I'd go. I could find a job in Vegas pretty easily, even without a letter of recommendation from her. What I really needed was to uphold the promise I'd made my father, though. I told him I'd stay with Agatha, and take care of her.

What would he have done if he'd known how badly she would treat me? She regarded me as a servant since I had nothing to my name. I lived in a tiny room in the loft. I worked from the time the sun rose until the sun set, making sure the business was running smoothly, and it was a rare day indeed that I took off.

I sighed wistfully. No matter how much I wanted to escape her, I could never live with myself knowing that I'd gone back on my word to my father.

I stared at their retreating figures for a moment before I turned back to where Ruby waited.

I needed information. Ruby would fill me in. And I could trust her to keep a secret, too.

"Ruby," I said, sliding her tea next to her and glancing around, making sure Agatha and her daughters were gone.

"Tell me everything you know about this dance? Who are the Villanovas?"

CHAPTER SEVEN

I lifted the glass of wine and sipped it, grimacing. Wine wasn't my thing, but my mom liked it, and when I spent time with her we often shared a bottle.

"In two days, things are going to change, son," she said, looking through the open glass doors to the study. We sat on the balcony overlooking the garden below, the heat of the day diminishing now that the sun was set. I owned a penthouse a few blocks away, but never spent much time there, between work and the various tasks my father had me do. This was my childhood home, ridiculously lavish. My mother took a sip, swallowed, and sighed. "I knew this day was coming, but hoped things would be different."

I swallowed the cool, sour drink before placing the glass down, wishing it gave me liquid courage like it once did. But no, now I was immune.

"What made you think things could be different?" I asked curiously.

She shook her head sadly. She looked a lot like me, the same blondish hair, the same hardened look in her eyes. "I hoped maybe you'd have taken a different course. And no, I'm not blaming you. I just wish you'd have found a wife by now, someone you truly cared about, and he wouldn't have to do it for you. When he does it for you, it's a far scarier circumstance."

She was admitting this, then. I looked at her with interest as I sipped my chardonnay. "Scary?" I asked, then snorted. "I don't see anything scary at all about an anonymous ball in which I choose my future. What could be scary about that?"

She looked at me with pursed lips, silently asking me not to do this, to make it easier on her.

I looked away. I didn't want to meet her eyes. Maybe it was my silence that gave me away, or maybe my father had already tipped her off.

"Oh my God. You do have someone," she said softly. "Dante, look at me." I did, reluctantly, draining my glass before I met her eyes.

"Yeah?"

"You've met someone, haven't you?" she whispered.

I shook my head and looked away.

"You sure about that? People say otherwise." Her voice took on a sharp edge, and it pissed me the fuck off.

I rose. "So now you're spying on me, too?" I asked coolly. "Why'd you ask me if you already knew?"

"No. For God's sake, Dante, sit." I did not want to sit.

Finally, with a sigh, she continued.

"Listen, all I mean is that you don't have to do this. If you already have a woman, then there's no need for us to go through with this ridiculous ball. Really, honey. Stop being so secretive about her, and all of this will go away."

I shook my head. Had she completely convinced herself of a lie? "What goes away, Mom? The control the Villanova family has over the entire state? The way we manipulate everyone and anyone who gets in our way?" Was she delusional?

Her eyes begged me to be merciful. "No, that's not what I mean—" she continued but I interrupted.

"Nothing goes away. The only choice I have is whether or not I go to this goddamned masquerade and choose a wife, and pretend I never met the woman I did, or I bring her into the family. So yeah," I said with a forced bark of laughter. "You're right. There is no real choice. Not when she means something to me. Not when I want to keep her protected from all of this, keep her safe and out of the fray." I turned my back to my mother, and she didn't say anything for a little while. She didn't need to. She was a smart woman and knew I spoke the truth.

"You're a good man, Dante," she said, and her broken tone surprised me. I turned to her, startled. Was she crying? "A good man to want to protect her from—this." She waved her hand around the study, but I knew better. I knew what she was talking about.

The control. The violence.

The fear.

"I'm not a good man," I denied. I was under no delusion... I knew who I was. Sighing, I ran a hand through my hair as I got to my feet. "Listen, I need to go out for a while." I needed to get out of the oppressive heat of this room, the pressure that threatened to choke me.

My mother rose as well. "Do you know anything about her, Dante? Anything at all?"

I ran a hand across my face and through my hair. "She's a waitress," I said with a mirthless laugh. "One of, what, ten thousand in Vegas?"

My mother sighed.

"And even if I did know, I'd do well to forget," I said, shaking my head.

"Do you need me to get you a tux?" she asked as I walked away.

"I have four. I'll find one that'll do." I swallowed my anger as I left the room, at the thought of what I had to do, the final acceptance that anything good and true would never be mine. I looked at the clock.

One hour until midnight.

I walked out the door and wondered, where would she be? How would I find her? I needed to see her, to talk to her... but if I did, every second that I spent with her would be that much closer to exposing her to my family, and that couldn't happen. Even my mother in all her interest in keeping me safe didn't want to see that happen.

I had some time to kill so I drove to where we'd meet. I waited. And I waited some more.

I looked at the time on my phone. She was thirty fucking minutes late.

"Dante?" My stomach flipped in recognition and I smiled to myself before I turned to face her. Jesus, what that girl did to me. Her wide green eyes look up with me in eager antici-pation, her gorgeous smile making me warm inside as it was directed at *me*. She still wore her name badge and an apron tied around her waist. My lips quirked as I tugged on the string and it fell into my hands. She flushed, the pretty glow of her cheeks warming me.

I wanted to ask her where she'd been, why she was late, if she was okay... but the only words that came out were, "Wanna go for a ride?" My voice sounded hoarse. She grinned, but then her face fell and she looked back over her shoulder.

"If I'm gone too long tonight, she'll miss me, and she's in a mood," she whispered.

"And if she misses you?" I asked.

She stared at me a good long while and bit her lip before her eyes glanced around her again. "She won't miss me for a little while. Maybe an hour."

I grinned at her. "An hour will do. Get on the bike, babe."

I held it for her and she swung herself up, wrapped her small hands around my waist and I kicked up the engine.

"So how was your day?" she yelled into my ear as I pulled onto the highway as if we were sitting having coffee and not sneaking away into the darkness. I could hardly hear her at all.

I chuckled. So sweet. "Day's better now that I've got you here," I said, realizing even as the words left my mouth how stupid they sounded, but I didn't fucking care.

She rolled her eyes. "Well, I haven't showered yet, so don't be so sure."

"We can arrange to fix that, you know," I teased and she giggled against my back, a soft laugh that made my heart thump and my cock twitch.

"Where are we going?" she asked.

"Does it matter?"

No. No it didn't matter, not a bit, and we both knew it.

I was going where we'd have a little peace.

We rode in silence, but the quiet seemed nice and natural, not forced. My phone buzzed, but I ignored it. I knew I had to be back. I knew my father was expecting me to close a deal, and soon, and if it didn't go as planned, I'd have to make what my father called "a tough choice."

"I'd hate to see anyone hurt," he'd lied, his lips betraying his greed as the quirking of his mouth showed exactly how he really felt. It was what he always said, right before he ordered someone's leg broken, a house ransacked, a trigger pulled. He'd said it so many times it'd become expected... the calm before the storm.

There were "tough choices" to be made working for him, but I'd already made the most difficult one of all, and now I was flirting with danger. *You can do this,* I told myself. *You can protect her from the rest of them.*

"Here," she shouted in my ear. "Why don't we stop here?"

I smiled to myself. "Is that how a good girl asks?" I teased.

I felt her smile right down in my gut as she breathed in my ear. "Please, Daddy? Can we take this exit?"

"Anything you want, baby," I said, warming at her words. I took the exit and found us meandering down a road that led to a park surrounded by trees, with a trail before us lined with picnic tables. During the day it might've been crowded but it was vacant at night and thankfully, lit by moonlight.

"Perfect!" she exclaimed.

I scanned the park until I saw a secluded bunch of trees. From there, I'd see anyone who followed us. I parked the bike and put up the kickstand, holding it steady while she got off, then me, and I took her by the hand, glancing around us.

We didn't say anything at first. We didn't need to.

I pulled her to me and kissed her forehead, holding her close for a moment before I released her. I led her to the trees and sat down, pulling her onto my lap as I did. She snuggled up to me, nestled her head against my chest, and her little hand held onto my shoulder.

"Perfect," she said with a contented sigh. "I wish it didn't have to be so rushed or secretive. But I know I can't stay for long, and neither can you. Did you ever wonder what would happen if we just said... *fuck them*! You know? If you just said, hey, this is my girl and I said, I'm with him, and everyone would just have to get over themselves and we'd be who we needed to be without having to worry about what other people would do?"

I smiled, my mind stuck on the words *this is my girl*, but I needed to move past that. "Did you just say a naughty word?"

She flushed, her face hot against the bare skin at my neck. "I don't usually say curse words," she said.

"Uh oh," I tsked, pulling her up on my chest and giving her a stern look as I took her chin between my fingers. "You were a very bad girl. Does Daddy need to punish you?"

She shook her head from side to side. "Nooo?" she said, hopeful despite her protest.

"Then you need to behave yourself," I said, "unless you want to be taken across Daddy's knee. Do you?" I asked.

This time, she hesitated before answering, "No!" I pushed her to the side and smacked her ass, hard. She gasped and got even closer to me.

"Come here," I said, taking her back in my arms and kissing her. I pulled away just long enough to whisper, "I missed you, Gabriella. I've been thinking about you all day. God, I'm glad you're back." And before I could kiss her again, she took my face in her hands and pulled my mouth to hers. She kissed with a passion that belied her innocence. My cock stirred. After a while, she let me go and settled back down on my lap.

"Jesus, woman," I groaned. "What the hell was that?"

She lowered her lashes and clucked her tongue. "Now who's the one using bad language? Maybe you're the one who needs to be punished." She couldn't even keep the giggle out of her voice as she pretended to scold me.

"Yeah, I don't think so," I said, gently pushing her off my knee so that she lay flat on her back in the grass, her wide green eyes blinking up at me in shock as I took both her wrists and pinned them to the ground, holding her down as I towered over her. God, I loved the feel of her beneath me like this, innocent and helpless, like I could do anything I fucking wanted. "Doesn't work like that, baby."

"Oh?" she asked, her brow furrowing. "So this is a double standard, then," she said, shaking her head. "I do what you say or you punish me, but you can be as... potty mouthed and... bossy as you want?"

"Exactly."

I lowered my mouth and trailed my tongue down the side of her neck before I whispered. "Total fucking double standard." I took her lobe in my mouth and bit down, causing her to squirm and moan.

A twig snapped, and I nearly released her. My instincts were immediately on alert, my senses awakened, as I stared around me. Had someone followed us? Were they onto me? I was never alone, never truly private. But to my surprise, a tiny brown-nosed deer stood just a few feet away, staring at us.

"Don't move," she whispered. "They startle so easily."

I froze, still holding her thin wrists in my hands, feeling her pulse on my palms as the wide-eyed doe stared at us, unmoving, so pretty, like something out of a fairy tale.

"Is that Bambi?" I whispered, and she snorted so loud it startled the deer. It turned and fled.

I shook my head sadly at Gabriella. "You told *me* not to startle it, and look at you," I scolded. "You really are trying to earn that punishment, aren't you?"

She grinned but didn't reply.

"C'mere," I said, pretending to be gruff but really wanting to hold her close, because my heart still hammered in my chest from thinking we were being followed.

She burrowed against me as if she belonged there, her hand snaking around my waist and holding tightly.

"I'm tired," she admitted. "Worked so hard today. We had a school group come in for the lunch buffet, a party of businessmen from Japan who legit spoke no English, so I kept messing up their orders and they got mad at me and didn't leave me a tip. And then I spilled an entire five-gallon bucket of freshly made lemonade because I saw a mouse, a *mouse*, Dante, and I screamed and my stepmother was sooo mad at me she said she was gonna dock my pay even though lemonade costs, what, a dollar to make?" She sighed. "And my step sisters were going on and on about this... ball or dance or something that they want to go to."

That got my attention. "Oh yeah?" I asked, running my hands through her hair. "And babe, your stepmother sounds like a bitch."

She grunted. "Not gonna disagree with that. She sure can be."

I held her against me and kept running my fingers through her hair, so soft and warm and fragrant, it soothed me, doing this. I hated that she'd been overworked and mistreated and there wasn't a fucking thing I could do about it.

"So what's this... ball or dance you're talking about?"

Could it be...?

"It's like... a masquerade or something. People have to wear masks and dress up, and rumor has it that it's got something to do with the big family here in Vegas. You know the family that runs everything? The *mob*?"

"The Villanovas?" I asked, my voice sounding too gruff, hollow even, but she didn't seem to notice. I swallowed hard. "Yeah. I've heard of them."

A cold feeling coiled its way in my belly. Somehow, naming them—naming *us*—made it all too real. "Yeah, I've heard of them," I repeated.

How long could I hide who I really was from her?

"So what about them?" I asked

"Ruby says they've done some very bad things but they're not all bad *people*," she said.

I liked Ruby already.

"Yeah? And who's this Ruby chick?"

Gabriella snorted and slapped her palm on my chest. "She isn't a chick. She's like really, really old. She's my most dedicated customer at the restaurant, and a really good friend to me."

I definitely liked Ruby.

"Is she a girl?"

"She's a woman! All grown up."

"Then she's a chick."

"Chicks are younger girls."

"Not to me. You've got tits and curves, you're a chick."

"You did not just say that."

"Oh, I did," I said, not able to stifle my chuckle. She reached her hand out to playfully smack me but I nabbed her wrist and lowered my voice. "What'd I say about that?" I said, allowing my tone to grow harsher.

She froze and buried her head on my chest. "Sorry," she whispered.

She liked me being her daddy. I could see it in the way her chest rose and fell and her eyelids fluttered.

"It's okay, babe," I soothed, tucking her hair behind her ear. "Now tell me what happened with your step sisters." She looked up at me and nodded.

"Nothing happened, really. We talked about the masquerade thing, and they fought and caused a scene because they aren't always very nice people, and that was about it. Ruby told me that the masquerade would be a big deal but only the elite would be invited, so it didn't really matter to me anyway."

I didn't want to talk about this. My stomach twisted and my hands clenched into fists. Everyone would be toasting the son of the king. There would be dancing and food and drink, but it was not a celebration. It was a death sentence. When I found the woman I would wed for life, I would have to be faithful, no matter who she was. I was a bastard, but I'd seen enough of the misery my father had caused my mother to know that I would never cheat on the woman I one day gave my name to. I would have to say goodbye to Gabriella, to her innocence and purity and goodness, and commit myself to my family, to the darkness, forever. And it was then, while I held her, the moonlight reflecting on her beautiful golden hair, her little hand innocently splayed on my chest in a show of trust and vulnerability, I knew that I'd been harboring hope. That somehow, I'd escape the darkness. That somehow, I wouldn't be mired in it. That I'd find a way to cleanse my soul of the sins I'd committed, of the blood on my hands that wouldn't wash off.

I'd never admitted it to myself, but I'd somehow convinced myself that being single meant I could alter the future of the Villanova family, but I knew it was a lie. I stood no more chance of affecting change than a sea wall did of stopping a roaring monsoon. I was the son of the king, but even so, I was a pawn. A fucking pawn.

"What's the matter, Dante?" she asked, and her face tilted up to mine. Her large green eyes looked at me with such trust and concern that my throat tightened.

"Nothing, baby," I lied, forcing a smile.

She shook her head. "You tensed up just now. I could feel it, as if you were afraid or angry about something." She touched a finger to my cheek and brushed the scruff there. "You hold sadness in you, and I wish I could take it away. What weighs on you so much, Dante?"

I shook my head. No, I couldn't tell her. She could never know.

"I don't want to talk about it, Gabriella," I said. "Our time is short. Not tonight, babe."

Not *ever*.

She blinked and stared at me before she nodded, and rested her head back up against my chest. I had to change the subject. "Tell me about Ruby. Who is she? And why is she a good friend to you?"

"Ruby is a widow. She was married to her husband for like, decades, Dante. *Decades.* They got married after the war, which by now seems so far away. They were just young, she was twenty-one like me. Her husband was older, like you." I grinned. I was only thirty. "He was like an investor or real estate agent or something like that. But he became super rich. Maybe even like a millionaire. She could afford to have a personal chef come and maybe live in her home and cook for her, but she comes to us instead. I'm not exactly sure why."

I snorted. God, the girl could talk.

"Yeah, baby. She could. And she likely does, sometimes, you know. But I could make a pretty educated guess as to why she comes, and that reason is lying right here in my arms."

She quieted then. "You're just teasing me," she finally whispered.

"I'm not teasing you," I said, my voice hardening.

"Yes, you are," she said back to me, her tone growing argumentative.

What the hell?

I sat up and pulled her up with me so that she would turn around and face me. "Gabriella, what are you talking about?" I asked. "I'm dead serious. I don't know this Ruby person so I won't presume to know her motivations, but I do think there's a really good chance the reason why she's there every day is because of *you.*"

She blinked and shook her head.

"Don't deny it, honey," I said to her. "You're sweet and charming and funny. Why wouldn't she come just for you?"

She sighed and looked away. "Well. Okay, fine, maybe she

does enjoy me. I certainly enjoy her. In any event, Ruby was married for decades."

So she wanted to change the subject. Fair enough. I could understand that.

"And then her husband had a heart attack and died. Dante, it was the saddest thing I'd ever heard, her telling me this story. She talks about him with so much love, though. Says he was generous and funny and bossy, and that she loved that he was because she always felt safe around him."

She smiled shyly. "And I understand *all* of that."

I held her close and nodded.

"Dante, can you even imagine? Marrying someone and loving them like that? Knowing them for decades? For like longer than you *didn't* know them? It's funny how the world works, how two people living separate lives just meet. Is it by chance or fate or accident? I don't know... But I have thought about Ruby and her husband so many times. How she must've felt losing him. I've only known you for such a short time, and already..." Her voice trailed off, but I didn't need her to continue. I got what she was saying. Closing my eyes, I drew her close.

"Yeah, it's hard to imagine love like that, huh?" My voice was oddly husky, and hers was, too.

"She still wears the wedding band he gave her." She grew silent, and I didn't feel the need to fill in the gaps then. It felt nice being quiet, just the two of us like this. After a few minutes, she spoke up again. "My mom and dad were like that, you know." Her voice was almost a whisper.

"Yeah?" Mine weren't, but she didn't need to know that.

"Tell me about them," I said, holding her against me. My back had begun to ache a little, and I was thirsty, but I didn't want to move. Not now. Not ever. It was cool and quiet here, and we were alone. I knew our time was coming to an end, but I'd keep her as long as I could. I wanted to hear her speak. It was enough, just listening to her soft voice as she shared her innermost thoughts with me, just seeing her fingers entwine with mine. Soft. Secret. Special.

"They met in high school," she began, then she paused with a little laugh. "Mom said that Dad was the one who teased her the most, and Dad said it was only because he wanted the other boys to stay away from her."

"Understandable," I interjected.

"And then I guess she grew to tolerate his teasing," she said with a laugh. "Dad was ruthless, she said. She used to tell me the story of the time he tied her shoes together during science class and when she stood, he placed himself right in front of her so she fell straight into his lap."

I chuckled. "That's sort of brilliant, actually. Tried and true but with a twist." As I spoke, I wove my fingers through her hair, so soft. She closed her eyes briefly and sighed. Just holding her like this, I wanted more. Her sigh reminded me of her moans in the hotel room. I swallowed hard, trying to focus on what she said. I needed her alone again. Resting my hand on her neck, I encouraged. "Go on."

She pulled closer to me. "So they married right out of high school. Mom got pregnant with me before she even graduated. Her mother didn't approve of dad, but she was old-fashioned enough to want to see her married. And Mom and Dad didn't care. Looking back now, as an adult, I could see how hard it must've been for them. Dad worked hard, but always made time for us."

I admired that. A dad who was busy with his work but made time for his family.

"I want to be a dad like that," I said. Something about being around her made me speak things I wouldn't tell other people.

"Well," she said, her voice taking on an edge of the pragmatic, "If you want it badly enough, you will have it."

She was so fucking naïve. "Go on," I said.

She snuggled in closer. "I love that you want to be a dad like that," she whispered. She didn't know, though. She didn't know that I would never have children, never bring them into a family like mine.

"Tell me more about your parents," I prodded. I needed to hear her speak. I needed to hear what normal, loving families were like.

"Oh, there isn't much more to tell," she said. "Mom liked to cook, so she cooked for us even though dad owned a restaurant. She would bake cookies with me, and we'd sing together. And then one day, she just couldn't sing anymore."

Her fingers tightened in mine, and her voice took on a sad edge.

"What happened?" I asked.

"She was sick," she whispered, and I felt her tremble a bit then. I almost stopped her. She didn't need to tell me this part.

Or did she?

"Yeah?" I asked, letting my arms tighten just a bit more around her.

"She had a heart condition. When I was very young, they tried some treatments that weren't very effective, and I remember thinking she would get better any day, but she didn't. She gradually grew worse and worse. Then one day when I came home from school, she was gone. Just gone. Dad told me she'd died, and we went out and walked around mom's favorite garden, and picked daisies and put them in a vase. I cried, but not in front of him. He had enough grief of his own."

I could see her now, my courageous little girl, her chin lifted high as she braved facing what had to have been the most tragic moment of her life. Selfless, even as a child.

"How old were you?" I asked quietly.

"Ten." The words hung in the air. I wanted to go back in time and hug the little girl who lost her mom and put on a brave face for her father.

"Ten," I repeated. "Ten-year-olds should be doing fun things, like riding bikes and playing with their friends."

Not that I knew.

I was ten when I witnessed my first hit, someone who'd betrayed my father. It hadn't been planned. Even my father likely would have shielded me if he'd known. But I was there when my father's hired man pulled the trigger. I screamed in horror at the splatter of blood on the wall behind the man, the way his eyes went from shocked to vacant, and how my father's men hadn't even flinched. Later that night, my dad found me sleeping curled up next to my mom, dragged me into my own room, and told me it was time to be a man.

"He'll need to see," he explained to my mother the next day. "There's nothing we can do about this. He'll need to see."

I could still hear the words, still feel my mother sitting next to me on my bed, tucking me in when my father had gone back out.

Gabriella had said something but I hadn't heard her, I'd been so mired in my own memories.

"What's that?"

"So what was your childhood like?" she asked.

I chose not to respond but merely shrugged. "That's for another day," I told her. "Why don't you tell me how your father met your stepmother. I want to know. How does someone marry a woman like that?"

She laughed and shook her head. "I'm not sure," she whispered. "I think that it was... something to do with business. But he died soon after they married. She says my father left her destitute and in debt, so I owe it to her to work for the family business, to make up for his debt."

"That's ridiculous," I said, my anger rising. I wanted to

shake the woman who took advantage of her like this. "You're an adult now, Gabriella. You could leave at any time."

"But my father said to take care of her," she whispered. "And she told me that he left her in huge debt, that it was only out of the goodness of her heart she provided for me, that she owes me nothing. So... I do it for him, not for her."

I closed my eyes briefly.

Fucking hell. Of course she did.

"I don't understand why he married her," she said. "If it was for money, I'd rather have been dirt broke." She laughed a little then but it rang hollow. "I mean, I already am. It isn't half bad."

I wouldn't know.

"Dirt broke?" I asked, and she looked up at me.

"Does that bother you?"

"Of course not," I said. "I would never judge you for something like that. It just bothers me that you have to struggle at all. I wish that I could fix things for you. So... define dirt poor," I said. "You have food to eat? A place to sleep?"

She looked away and I shook her a little. "Answer me, Gabriella," I said sternly. "I need to know."

She finally looked back up at me. "I have everything I need," she said. "Just not much else. They need me to work every day and so I do. I clean our house. I do the laundry. I have always done whatever was necessary to earn my keep." She paused. "Our time's almost up, Dante," she whispered regretfully. "I have to go back now. And you barely kissed me."

Her eyes teased me, and she turned to face me. I grinned at her. I wanted to do a fuck of a lot more than kiss her.

With a tug, I pulled her close, and brought her mouth to mine. If she wanted a kiss, I'd give her a fucking kiss.

Her lips parted and I slipped my tongue in, probing her

soft, sweet mouth as I did, and her little whimpers made my cock harden as I held her. This was what I needed, and I could tell from her response she needed it, too, the way her body melted into mine and she held on tighter, as if she needed to get closer. I deepened the kiss, laying her gently down so that I was over her, but not breaking contact, her gentle moan stirring something in me. I needed more. But our time was short, and we were in the middle of nowhere. I heard another twig snap, and the spell was broken. Fully expecting another deer, or some other wild creature, I looked into the woods but saw nothing.

"What was that?" she whispered. "Just... another deer?"

"I don't know. But it's time to go."

"Okay." I reached for a lock of her hair and tugged it a little.

She gasped, as I whispered, "Is that how you talk to me, little girl?"

She closed her eyes briefly, swallowing, before she answered, "Yes, Daddy."

"That's a good girl," I said as we stood and made our way back to the parking lot.

Who would my dad have sent after me? Was it one of his men, or one of my enemies?

"Is everything ok, Dante?"

No, of course it wasn't okay, but I wouldn't tell her that. Were we found out? Not yet, no, and when we had the fucking ball I'd find someone to appease him and then yeah, everything would be fine.

It'd be fucked up and I'd never be happy again, but she'd be safe.

"We're fine, babe," I said. "You ok?"

"Of course I am," she said. "I'm very happy when I'm with you. I'm not really sure why but I am. I do need to get back now."

"Let's go," I said. "Gotta get you to bed so you can get to Ruby in the morning."

She smiled. "Of course. She'd like you, you know."

She wouldn't, but Gabriella didn't need to know that.

"You think? She's got a thing for guys with tattoos?" I asked wryly.

She laughed outright at that, her head tossing back as she giggled her little head off. I grinned.

"How did you know?" she said. "She's always all about the guys with tattoos. Likes 'em rough and tattooed."

"And young?" I asked. The woman had to be old enough to be my grandmother.

The woods rang with her peals of laughter once again, and I looked around me sharply.

No movement. No sound.

Though I scanned the trees, there was no evidence of anything at all. Nothing but the light rustling of wind through the leaves, and the faintest sound of an owl hooting.

And then I heard it. Another crack. I stiffened and pulled Gabriella to me, but her foot caught on something as she went tumbling away from me, her hands splayed out in front of her.

"Gabriella!" I yelled, then wished I hadn't. God, if anyone heard me call her name...

I grabbed her, but it was too late, she'd already gone sprawling onto the concrete. I lifted her in my arms and inspected her scraped hands. "You okay, baby?" I asked. I hated that she'd hurt herself like this and wished I could take the pain away.

"God, I'm such a klutz," she whispered. "Such a klutz! Look, my hands are a mess," she moaned.

"Jesus, baby," I said, taking each hand and kissing each injured palm, not caring that her blood stained my lips, only needing to bring solace. "I'm so sorry I didn't catch you."

"I'm fine," she said. "Really, I'm fine. Let's just go now."

I grabbed the little first aid kid I kept with me, cleaned her palms, and bandaged them. When I was done, I kissed her bandaged hands, gave her a quick hug, and pulled her on the bike. Her arms wrapped around my middle, and I kicked the engine to life. I had to get her to safety.

CHAPTER EIGHT

*T*he wind whipped through my hair as we traveled on the highway together. There was no casual banter this time, no screaming into the wind to be heard. I held tight, and he drove fast.

I didn't know exactly what had happened back there, but I knew that something wasn't right. His body stiffened beneath my hands as we drove, but I was so focused on how badly my hands stung that I could think of little else. It hurt like hell. God, I was such a klutz. He didn't seem to mind though.

He'd kissed my hands and bandaged them.

I closed my eyes as we drove, until the lights grew brighter and the sounds louder, and we rolled into the busy, bustling late night downtown on the strip.

He brought his bike to a stop, his booted feet coming to the ground, before he turned to speak to me over his shoulder.

"Your hands, babe," he said. "They okay?"

I nodded but I was lying. "They're fine."

One quick nod and he took my hands to his lips again. I

melted a bit as he gently lifted me down from the bike, leaned over, wrapped a hand around my neck, and kissed me.

"Tomorrow," he whispered in my ear before releasing me. "Meet me at midnight."

That was our thing, then.

Meet me at midnight.

"Yeah?"

I nodded, overcome with strange emotions I couldn't decipher. "Yeah," I said, then I smiled at him. I'd give this much to him. "Yes, Daddy."

His eyes crinkled around the edges and his lips quirked.

"Where do you live?" he asked, one brow raised as he looked around, but it wouldn't be possible for him to see that I lived in the most run-down apartment in the neighborhood.

"Over there." I pointed in the general direction of the higher-end apartments, hoping he wouldn't hone in on my vagueness. He didn't.

He leaned into me, and I tugged on his beard, the coarse, blondish brown hair making me shiver. He captured my fingers, kissed them to his lips, and released me. Then he bent down and smacked my ass, hard, before he kicked up his bike and took off. A goodbye spank. I smiled to myself.

When he was gone, I turned to go home, I was just a few paces from where he'd left me, when shadows crept around me. I realized after a short while that I wasn't alone.

Why were they following me? What did they want?

I only had a few paces left now, so I walked even faster when one of them spoke.

"What's the rush, honey? Where are you going?"

I would not engage. No, I would not speak to them. Reaching in my bag, I wrapped my fingers around the cold, hard edges of my keys. Maybe I could use them as a weapon if I had to, stab them with the sharp metal or something if they attacked.

These guys wanted more. I could feel it in my gut.

My keys jangled in my hands as I turned the corner. Our apartment building was so close I could see it now, but I gasped and yelped as one of the strangers following behind me raced in front of me and blocked my path.

"Such a pretty little thing," he drawled. His face was cloaked in darkness, the shadows preventing me from seeing him fully, all I could make out was a tall, gangly form, and greedy little eyes.

"Very pretty little thing," agreed a second man, who stood to the side of the first. He was heavier. Bigger. Scarier.

Perhaps I could disarm them. "Oh, hello, gentleman," I said. "How nice to make your acquaintance. Now would you be good enough to step aside so I can go home now? My brother and father are likely back home from their shifts at the police station. Both cops, you know. And it's time for me to get upstairs. Anything you were looking for?"

When the creeps in front of me chuckled, a sliver of fear tingled along my spine.

"You lie," the heavier man said, his eyes darker now. "We know who you are. We know where you're going. You don't have a brother, and your father died three years ago."

Cold, sick, dreadful fear came over me then. Who were they?

"What do you want?" I dropped all manner of civility.

"Wanna know who you were with," one guy said. "That's all. You were gone a while and we're tracking someone. We want to know who you are and why you're with him."

"That's none of your business," I said.

Who were they? I wished Dante was with me. They wouldn't bother me if he was.

"None of our business?" the taller guy said, and they all closed in on me. "Seems when it's four against one, everything's our business, sweetheart. Now tell us, before we have to do something we regret."

I stood mutely. What would I tell them anyway? His name was Dante. That was all I knew.

One man reached out and grabbed my hair, yanking my head back, at the same time another reached for my purse. I yelled at both of them, furiously angry, stomping my feet and trying to pull away, but neither would budge.

A rumble of a motorcycle froze them in place. "Go!" one shouted, but they were too late, the beam of Dante's headlights swinging into view. The man let go of my hair tried to run, but Dante swung in front, blocking his escape. I fell back, watching in fascination and fear. What would he do?

He grabbed one guy by the scruff of his shirt, kneed him hard and when the man tried to stand, Dante leveled him with one vicious blow. Then he turned to the man who'd had me by the hair, grabbing the hem of his shirt as the man tried to run.

"You dare to lay your fucking hands on a woman? *My* woman?" he hissed. He hit him so hard the man's head snapped back. I didn't want to watch, but I couldn't look away, at the terrifying form of Dante, *my* Dante, defending my honor. The man's face was bloodied and swollen but still, Dante did not stop until the man collapsed to the ground. "Get your asses out of here and don't you ever set foot near her again, or I'll fucking kill you."

"Are you alright?" he demanded, glancing down at me, his eyes aflame and his brows furrowed, his hand on my neck so tight it almost hurt.

"I-I'm fine," I said, my voice shaking, and the sound seemed to somehow shake him out of his fury. He exhaled hard, and tugged me toward his chest. I burrowed in, needing to feel his strength.

"Thank God," he said, then he released me and tossed his

head back, his hands fisted by his side. "I fucking hate this. Hate this!" he hissed, his beautiful brown eyes tortured.

"You hate what?" I whispered, trembling now that he'd saved me. I was unharmed, but still shaken up by it all. I reached for his shoulder, but he shook me off.

"I hate that you aren't safe." He paced, running a hand through his hair. "I hate that I can't even drop you off without wondering if you are gonna get hurt."

"What do you mean?" I said, apprehension prickling my spine. "Those were just random guys who wanted to get a rise out of me. Pick on the innocent-looking girl." I shrugged. "Happens all the time."

He sobered then, his eyes narrowing on me. "Does it?"

Oh, Jesus. "I'm... well... it happened before. Though... they said they wanted to know who I was with," I finished weakly.

He shook his head and swore. "And where the hell are you?" he barked. "This isn't where you said you lived. This is ridiculous, Gabriella."

I felt a bit guilty then. "Well, I didn't want you to see where I live," I said, my voice dropping, as I chipped away at the concrete with the toe of my sneaker. He glared at me, hands anchored on his hips, and I had to look away.

"Dante, I need to go," I pled. "She'll be looking for me."

Tough as he was, something in his gaze flickered. "Yeah. Me, too."

"So wait a minute. How'd you even know I was being followed? I thought *you* were going home?"

"I was," he said with a sheepish shrug of his shoulder. "I wanted to be sure you were safe, so I watched you."

"You spied on me? Oh that isn't creepy at *all*!"

It wasn't, really, but I wanted to needle him a little.

He narrowed his eyes again. "It isn't creepy. I was worried about you. It's late, and you're just a little thing, and I was afraid people would take advantage of you. You're too damn innocent and naïve."

"Apparently I *am* if I didn't even know my boyfriend was following me!"

He blinked before I realized my error.

Um... I said boyfriend? My cheeks flamed.

"Yeah," he said and he glanced around briefly before looking at the time on his phone. "So this is where you really live?"

"Yeah," I said, wishing he'd go now. I didn't like him seeing where I lived.

He drew a bit closer and put his hand on the small of my back, causing me to look up at him. "Gabriella, I don't care where you live. Did you really think I did?"

We stood there in the quiet for a moment before I whispered, "I need to go."

He leaned in and touched his forehead to mine. "Me, too."

But neither of us moved.

I didn't want to say goodbye, not again. I still shook from the shock of what had happened. I wanted him to hold me, just a little while longer.

"Wish I didn't have to let you go, baby," he said, his voice low and husky. "Wish I could keep you here with me." His fingers interlocked with mine at the small of my back. "Gabriella, tomorrow, we'll spend the night together. Yeah?"

"Yeah," I whispered.

One curt nod, another fierce kiss on my forehead, and he whispered against the shell of my ear, his warm breath and whiskers making me shiver, "And tomorrow I'll punish you for lying to me."

I squirmed in both delicious arousal and apprehension, swallowing hard and said the only possible response. "Yes, Daddy."

He watched me go up the stairs that led to my apartment building. I could feel his eyes on me as I punched in the security code, and heard the faint click of the lock. I pushed the door open, and turned to look over my shoulder. He sat in the shadow of the streetlight, his arms crossed over his brawny chest, my beautiful, tortured, angry, sexy-as-hell Prince Charming. His hair hung over his forehead in sand-colored waves, his eyes trained on me, his jaw set in a firm line. The t-shirt stretched across his chest and his arms bulged at the biceps. Strong. Immovable. Fierce.

Mine.

I shivered with delight, as I stepped into the hallway, and as the door creaked shut, I felt cold hands on my shoulders. I opened my mouth to scream, but no sound came as a hand covered my mouth, and all I could hear behind me was the rumble of his bike as he drove away. My heart raced, my hands clammy. I recognized the lavender scent of my step-mother's perfume emanating from the warmth of the figure behind me. Tears watered my eyes. "Mmphh!" I said, struggling, trying to push her away, but her hands held fast.

"Where were you?" she hissed. "I called and you didn't answer. Where the fuck were you?" Her fingernails dug into the sensitive skin on my face, and I shook with fear. I tried to push her away, but she held me fast as she removed her hand from my mouth.

"I was out," I said. "And why can't I go out? I'm an adult and I'm not subject to your rules."

She spun me around to look at her, her eyes narrowed to mere slits as her jaw clenched in fury. She shook me, once. Then she let me go and stared.

"I suppose you're right," she said, her voice tight with anger. "But you're not my daughter."

I knew I wasn't and I didn't want to be, but I wasn't sure how to respond, so I just stared back.

"I hate calling you and getting no response. You're the manager of our restaurant and I expect that you'll answer your calls."

"At midnight?" I asked, my temper rising as I stepped closer to her. "And why did you think it okay to manhandle me just now?"

"I didn't want you to scream," she said, as if it were the most natural thing in the world to put your hand over the mouth of a fully-grown woman. She shook her head as if she had a sudden change of heart. I didn't trust her. I shook my head in disbelief as she continued. "But I'm sorry. I shouldn't have done that." she looked back out the window before looking back at me. "Who were you with? A boy?"

The thought of anyone calling Dante a boy was laughable.

I shrugged a shoulder. "Is it any of your business?"

I never spoke to her this way. My pulse still raced with fear, my anger at nearly being discovered putting me on edge.

"None of my business?" she asked with a raised brow, as she stepped closer to me. "None of my business?" Cold fear clawed at my belly. I knew this was the quiet before she'd snap, before she'd let loose the full rage she had for me. "You live under my roof, you tell me where you are and who you're with," she hissed, and her hand raised, as if to grab me, or smack me, but then she kept her hand frozen in mid-air and she stopped.

She smiled, but it sickened me. My stomach twisted as she tilted her head to the side. Something wasn't right...

"You know, you're right, sweetheart," she said, ending in a laugh that made my skin crawl. "You're so right. You're an adult. You owe me no explanation. If you want to spend your time with a man I don't know, or... whatever you're doing... I can't stop you. Lord knows I don't know where Violet and Elenora are half the time." She laughed another forced, half-crazed laugh. I held my breath. She was going to snap, and I didn't know what to expect when she did.

I said nothing as she continued. "I won't ask you again where you were. Just next time, be a dear and answer your phone, will you? Let me know where you are, Gabriella?"

"Yes," I said woodenly, staring at her, not quite knowing what to expect. "Certainly. I will. I'm sorry I didn't."

She nodded, then turned her back to me and walked toward the landing that would take her upstairs. Had she completely forgotten that she was angry with me?

"It's time you got some rest, and I did, too," she said. "After all, you're opening in the morning, aren't you?"

I wasn't but I knew this was my punishment. "Sure," I said.

That gave me four hours of sleep. Brilliant.

"Be sure you get there for inventory before we open, Gabriella. I must place the orders we need by noon tomorrow and I want to be sure the order is accurate."

I merely nodded. It was a four-hour job at best. She'd punish me with work, then, in a way that she could control.

We reached the top of the stairs, and she opened the door, ushering for me to go in. I went ahead of her, wishing she were in front of me. I knew that I didn't want her behind me. I needed to watch my back... literally.

The door clicked shut behind us. For some reason, my stomach clenched again, my breath becoming ragged.

What would she do?

I walked to my room and heard her walk to hers. I would not look back. I would *not*.

But as I shut and locked my door behind me, I couldn't help but feel Agatha had only just begun. Something terrible was going to happen, and I was powerless to stop it.

But as I slid under the covers, I remembered. I remembered how Dante looked, sitting astride his motorcycle, watching me go inside. The feel of his hand in mine, his fore-head pressed against mine, his warmth on every inch of my skin.

I was drunk on Dante, and I hardly even knew him.

I had to get away.

But how?

I made it to work in time, and went through early morning inventory. I comforted an employee who was distraught about a scheduled shift, and I brought Ruby her breakfast.

"Darlin', you look whipped," she said, shaking her head from side to side. Occasionally her southern roots surfaced and she lapsed into the vernacular.

Whipped. Heh. If she only knew.

"Sooo. Tired," I said, pushing her teacup to her on the table. "How are you?"

"Oh, I'm good," Rub answered, fixing me with a serious eye. "And why, pray tell, are you so tired? Anything I should know about?"

Ha. Only *everything*.

"Nah, it's nothing." I wanted to tell her about him so badly. I wanted her to know how insanely hot he was. I wanted to squeal with her about how well he treated me, and how he called me baby.

But it would be best if she did not know. She blinked, and then her face broke out into a slow, shit-eating grin. "Nothing?" she asked. "Sugar, you think I was born yesterday?"

I felt my cheeks flush with heat, and she stared at me. "Come here," she whispered, gesturing for me to bend over so she could whisper in my ear. "Is this the same gentleman caller as yesterday?"

Her old-fashioned phrases tickled me, but this time I just squirmed. I looked around me, knowing Agatha wouldn't be anywhere in the vicinity yet, but it felt as if the very walls were her spies.

"Hush, Ruby," I told her, looking around me wildly.

"Don't you hush me," she said. "I want you to tell me what's going on. I just want to know is all. Is that too much to ask for a little old lady? Hmmm?"

"Yes," I hissed, flicking open the menu and pointing to it. "Now tell me what you want for breakfast."

She laughed, and I watched as her wrinkled skin sagged around her mouth and lips, betraying her age, but her eyes were as young as ever. "It's Thursday, honey," she said. "Why would you ask me what I want for breakfast on Thursday?"

I blinked at her for a moment before it dawned on me. "I'm so sorry. I'm just tired today, Ruby. You want the stuffed pancakes with pecans and maple butter, and the strawberry compote on the side, right?"

She grinned. "Of course. You sure you don't have a good reason to be tired?" Her face fell a bit and I smiled at her for a moment. Fine, then. I leaned in closer.

"I do, Ruby," I whispered. "I do have a good reason. And I'll tell you everything but I have to wait until the time is right, okay?"

Her eyes met mine in solidarity before she nodded and patted my shoulder. "Of course, Gabriella. Now go get me my breakfast."

I flashed a smile, and trotted to go get her breakfast, but I froze when I entered the kitchen. My step sisters were leaning against the large, butcher-block table, poring over a catalog.

"I'll wear the green one," Elenora said. "It'll bring out the color of my eyes and hide my curves a bit. But I'll be cold in just that, so I'll need a shrug, too," she mused.

"I'll wear the red one," Violet chimed in. "I think it's bold and catches attention, and how else are we supposed to get the attention of the prince? For real?"

The prince? Well then. That was interesting.

I brought Ruby her breakfast and the morning went by quickly. With every minute that passed during the day, my heart lifted a little. It brought me closer and closer to seeing him.

I'd managed to forget the conversation I'd had with Agatha the night before. The truth was, I never did trust her, and I had no doubt she'd do something mean and vindictive when she had the chance, but her daughters had her occupied. I hoped that was enough for now. As I checked inventory at lunch and scrubbed the floor of the stock room, ignoring how my battered hands protested from such use, I heard Violet and Elenora rifling through the catalog again.

"Not those shoes," Elenora said. "God, Violet, you'll plummet to your death wearing those."

I sighed. Did those two ever work?

"I need height, though. I'm a shrimp and the prince is so tall." Violet's voice took on an ethereal, dreamlike quality that made me roll my eyes.

"As if you'll get anywhere near him," Elenora snorted, and I heard a smack and a rustling of clothing before Agatha's sharp, "Girls!" stilled the noise.

I shook my head to myself, as I broke down boxes in the corner and stacked them for the recycling. Would they ever grow up?

I jumped as someone banged on the door of the store room. "Are you coming out, or what?" Agatha barked. "We have customers out here waiting to be served dinner. Move it."

"I'll be right there," I yelled, as I straightened up the boxes she'd made me pile. I frowned. She'd asked me to check on the inventory, combine what we had and get rid of the boxes, and now she wanted me to wait the tables? Did she think I could bilocate?

I sighed to myself, as I looked heavenward. "Only for you, Dad," I said. I would do my duty, but that was all.

I opened the door and ignored the pang of jealousy that stung me as I walked past the open display of catalogs on the table in the kitchen, catalogs that glimmered with shoes and shrugs and shawls, heels and flats and platforms, clutches and handbags and wallets. They were shopping for the dance while I glanced down at my scuffed, worn flats, and walked on aching feet to serve those who waited. A little part of me wanted to be them. I wanted new, pretty things, and the chance to live a little, dream a little...

Then, I lifted my chin. Squared my shoulders.

I *would* dream. They couldn't take that away from me. But my dream was bigger than sequined clutches and killer heels. My dream rode a motorcycle, and tonight, he'd be waiting for me.

My silly thought made me giggle to myself. When I looked up, Agatha's eyes narrowed on me. What was that all about? She didn't like me laughing or smiling? I hurried past her and went to the first man waiting to be seated, a tall, thin guy a few years older than myself, his dark hair cropped short. He had one long, silvery scar that went from his jaw to his temple, and when his eyes met mine, they lingered a little too long.

My heartbeat kicked up a notch.

"May I help you?" I asked the man, grabbing a menu. "Just a table for one, sir?"

"Just one," he said, with a nod of cool geniality, but when his gaze fell to my hands, he froze, and he pointed at them. "What happened to your hands?" he asked. His gritty voice cut right through me. He seemed... lethal.

"Oh," I said with a forced laugh. "I just fell down is all." My voice shook with the little lie, but there was something about him that set me on edge.

"You fell?" he asked, as he followed me to a table at the back.

I nodded, ignoring the little voice inside me that said *run*, and seated him. "Right this way, sir. I'll be right with you."

"Thanks," he said, taking his seat, his eyes once more traveling to my hands, before he smiled at me, something behind that smile made me squirm.

"Would you like to hear our specials for tonight?" I asked, and when he nodded, I threw myself into prattling on about Bolognese and pappardelle noodles, cream of something soup, and midnight fudge chocolate cake.

He nodded, and opened the menu. "I'll take a look, thank you. For now, a glass of merlot, please."

I nodded and hastened to fulfill his order, before seating another half dozen people. When I came back with his wine, he'd neatly folded his menu on the table and was leaning back in his chair, observing his surroundings.

I took his order, and a feeling of unease once again anchored in my belly. I glanced at my phone. Nine thirty. A little squeal escaped me then when I realized I had less than three hours to see him. It didn't matter there was some creepy guy sitting at the table or that my sisters were buying out catalogs. Tonight, I'd be with Dante.

I maybe should have felt a bit guilty that he wasn't happy with me, but instead I just went about my work thinking over and over, "Tonight, Daddy's gonna spank me," with a suitable amount of repentance lest I actually think I was anticipating being punished.

But hell yeah, I actually was.

I served the man his meal, and when I slid the plate of

flank steak on the table in front of him, he looked up, frowning, and nodded his thanks.

"Anything else I can get for you, sir?" I asked as politely as possible.

"Yes," he said, lifting his cloth napkin and flicking it out in front of him. "The name of the owner of this restaurant?"

My belly flipped.

What?

His question startled me. "Agatha Reginald. Why?"

He nodded slowly, lifting his knife and fork into his hand. "No reason," he muttered, looking away and thereby dismissing me.

Later, when I went to bring him his check, I found that he'd left a one hundred dollar bill on the table. I blinked, picked the bill up, and looked around. His plate was clean, and he was nowhere to be found. Huh.

I shoved it in my apron pocket and glanced at the time, then smiled to myself. Just an hour before I'd get to see him.

When the clock struck just before midnight in the kitchen, I untied my apron and hung it up. My shift had ended an hour ago, but Agatha needed me to stay on a bit longer, so I had, and now I needed to get a move on if I was going to be on time to see Dante. But as I stepped to the door, a shadow crossed my path. I looked up in surprise to see Agatha standing there. "Going so soon?" she asked.

"Yes," I said with a nod. "Did you find everything you needed to order?" I fluffed my hair and glanced at the mirror that hung in the back. I supposed I looked fine. My eyes looked tired and my hair was a bit askew, but knowing I was meeting Dante made the color rise on my cheeks. I ran a lip gloss brush over my lips, and smiled at the reflection, until my eye caught Agatha's. She was staring. And she did not look happy.

"Order what?" she asked, her arms crossed over her chest.

"The dresses and shoes and whatnot," I said, making sure I had everything I needed in my bag before spinning around to talk to her.

She frowned at me "Yes. I overnighted everything. It'll be here tomorrow."

"Oh? Why overnighted?" I asked.

"The party is Friday night, Gabriella. The big masquerade."

When would I ever keep track of these things?

"Oh, right."

She smiled slowly, and I caught her wicked grin in the mirror behind me, making me shiver.

I blinked when I glanced at the time, I had five minutes. Even if I left now, I'd be late. Would I be in even worse trouble with Dante if I were tardy? What would he do? What would he say?

Daddy's gonna spank me.

But I had to get to him. I had to see where he was, and I had to reconnect. If I didn't...

"Would you mind looking at the clothes I picked out?" Agatha asked. "You don't have anywhere to go, do you? Could you give me a hand, maybe? It'll only take a second and then you can tell me if I ordered the right thing. Do you mind?"

I was now officially late, but resisting her would only make her angry, and if she suspected I was meeting someone, it could spell even more trouble.

Maybe he'd be late himself. Maybe he wouldn't even notice the time...

"Yeah, sure," I said. "Let's see them."

"Oh, I left the catalog in the store room," she said. "Can you grab it?"

Well that was weird. With a shrug, I headed to the store room, and glanced at the time on my phone. I had minutes now. Great. I tossed my phone on the desk. When I entered the room, it was dark, so I reached for the switch.

I didn't see Agatha. I never even heard her. But as I turned to flick the light, the huge steel door swung shut, clicking with an ominous snick. My breath caught in my throat as I tried the handle, but it was locked. I knew it would be. And even though I knew it was no use, I pounded on the door with my fists.

"Help!" I screamed. "I'm locked in here! Help! Please open the door!" But of course my pleas went unnoticed. I banged and screamed until my voice was hoarse, but no one came. I was locked in, with no way out.

CHAPTER NINE

$\mathcal{I}$ watched the pavement flash before me as I rode to meet her. Adrenaline pumped in my veins and eagerness to see her, to touch her, to feel her, filled every part of me. She was like a drug, and I needed my fix.

As was becoming my new routine, I'd ditched the suit and tie, welcoming the feel of the worn jeans and faded t-shirt that clung to me like a second skin. The day had worn on me, and I was ready for better things. I was sick of being mired in darkness. I needed to see my light.

Today, I'd had to be the heavy. The man who came in and cracked skulls. There had been a time when I'd reveled in it. I'd liked that people feared me when they saw me. I'd liked that they knew who I was. I'd liked the respect they gave me, the reverence in their voices, how they would give me the best seat in the house, the most expensive wine on the menu, preference over all others.

But now it sickened me. It wasn't respect born of integrity or hard work, but terror.

Today, I'd had to collect for my father. I'd made Beauregard, the man who owed my father, squirm beneath my glare, and pronounced his sentence while he begged for mercy. He hadn't heeded my first warning, the night I met Gabriella.

I wanted to vomit now, remembering his screams when they'd dragged him away to punish him, though he totally fucking deserved what he'd gotten.

Beauregard was a sick bastard. I was the son of the mafia lord and even I had never done something so repulsive. After confirming he was still using young girls and hadn't paid my father back, I'd given the orders to clear his store, send his associates home, and once I'd wrangled the truth from him, I'd ordered pain that would ultimately end in his demise, but not until he'd suffered.

We were powerful, and we were merciless. But even we didn't stoop that fucking low.

"We have our standards, Dante," my father would say. "We have our morals."

Fuck morals.

I pulled into the narrow street that brought me to the intersection where I'd meet her, but tonight, the air was different. There were the same people milling about, the same music piped through speakers overhead, bright lights that made it look far earlier than it really was. But... something was off. My instincts rose and I looked about me, searching for clues. I hadn't risen as respected commander of my father's army by accident.

My instincts were finely honed. A gift, my father said. I could smell betrayal a mile away.

And the yard where I was to meet her reeked of it. I took in my surroundings with deliberation, noting every detail, just a moment before the clock struck midnight.

No Gabriella.

I walked around looking for her, my gut telling me that

something was wrong. She'd been hurt. Someone had fucking hurt her, damn it. I had to find her. Where was she? I paced the narrow garden area, making sure I hadn't somehow missed her, that she wasn't sitting on a little bench waiting for me.

Where the fuck was she?

I peered by the trellis that overlooked the little man-made pond where lovers proposed and people threw coins into all day long. Nothing.

Fucking hell. I wanted her phone number. I needed to know she was okay. I needed to hold her. Where the fuck was she? As I paced, my concern grew to alarm level. I was gonna lose my mind. If she were anyone else... if I hadn't hidden who she was... I would call in assistance. We'd use every resource we had to scan every nook and cranny until we found her.

But hell, I didn't even have her fucking phone number.

God, I hated the secrecy and lies and sneaking around. I wanted to own this. Own *her*... in every way. But no... instead, I had to lift every rock in the fucking park to see if she was okay, to see if someone had hurt her. If Emilio had found her, if he knew who she was, and he knew that she was special to me...

Fuck the "traditional family values" bullshit. Fuck the whole "loyalty to the family" thing. I'd fucking kill him, bloodline be damned.

I glanced at my phone and realized she was twenty minutes late now, and my stomach seized. I knew in my gut she was in danger. God, what would I even do with myself? How could I handle her being hurt, or compromised in any way?

I paced around a small stone bench, ignoring a couple groping each other like lovesick teens. I walked past the old man feeding his dogs biscuits, and made my way to a clearing where a police officer paced. He caught my eye, and I knew he recognized me with the instinctive flare of his nostrils, intake of breath, then curt nod.

I ran a hand through my hair, frantic with worry, convinced that someone had found her out and hurt her. The thought of anyone touching her, of even looking at her... I'd fucking kill them.

But just as I'd made up my mind I would go on the hunt for her, I saw a gleam of golden hair, flying in the wind as she ran, and I stiffened. She was alive, and she was okay, and it looked as if she were unharmed.

Was she?

She ran around the corner, tripped, but caught herself, and I shook my head. Jesus. All we needed was for her to fall again, cause another injury, bring more unwanted attention to herself. But then she came into view, and my anger began to melt. God, she was beautiful. So fucking beautiful.

I wanted to scoop her into my arms and kiss every inch of her body, run my mouth along her collarbone and nip her skin, make her moan, and then I'd growl in her ear that she was daddy's little girl. My words would have the desired effect. Her breath would catch in her throat, her eyes would meet mine, and I'd promise to keep her safe, holding her close to me, close enough she could feel how much I loved her.

Then I'd turn her over my knee and spank her ass for making me worry like this.

"Gabriella," I whispered, holding my arms out to her, and when she came to me, I felt it. Someone was watching us, and not just strangers observing the happy reunion of two lovers. No. Someone with a far more serious agenda.

Fucking hell.

I pulled her to me, closing my eyes in thanks as her familiar scent, her soft hair, and her voice made me breathe a sigh of relief.

She was okay,

They hadn't found her. Not yet. And she was mine, at least for tonight.

"Sorry I was late," she said. "Oh my God. I got locked in our storeroom!"

I pulled away and looked down at her in shock. *"What?"*

"I had to look at a few things with my stepmother, and then the door shut and I couldn't get out. Were you waiting long?"

Waiting long? Was she fucking kidding me?

I put her at arm's length in front of me. "Gabriella, I was worried sick," I said, allowing my voice to take on a scolding tone as I fixed her with a stern look. "I looked all around the park, convinced that someone had hurt you. How did you get stuck in the storeroom?"

"It's the weirdest thing," she said, shaking her head. "I thought that Agatha had shut it on me, but she was gone when I came out, and I texted her. She said she thought I'd left and the door shut on its own. If the cleaners hadn't come..."

"You thought Agatha did it."

Not. Good.

"I can't imagine why she'd do such a stupid thing, though," she said, shaking her head.

I could.

"We need to go," I told her. "And we aren't coming back tonight. You're still okay with that?"

She smiled shyly. "Yes, Daddy," she whispered.

I paused a beat, needing to read her, knowing that was okay, and having to cool myself down. A few minutes ago, I'd been prepared to let her know she could never scare me like that again, and now I had to wonder if her stepmother had ulterior motives.

"Get on the bike, Gabriella," I said, grunting with impatience. I wanted out of here. "Let's go."

"You're mad," she said, her quiet, tremulous voice almost making me soften a little.

"I'm not mad." I held the bike while she got on and when she reached for me I looked at her hands, inspecting her to make sure she was okay. Her palms looked better, and I was pleased with that, though I was still furious, still shaking with the anger at her would-be attackers.

"You are," she whispered, her voice catching as she buried her head on my neck and I kicked up the engines. "Daddy's mad at me." Her voice shook and I wanted to make it better.

"I was scared because I thought you were hurt, baby," I said, gentling my tone. "I thought someone had hurt you, and I didn't know where I could find you or how to help."

"Wow," she breathed. "Just wow."

My lips quirked. Wow? She sounded like she'd just seen or heard something that completely astonished her.

"Yeah," she said breathlessly. "I... I just can't..." Her voice got a little high, a little shaky, as if she were going to cry. "Someone did before, just once before."

What was she talking about?

I sighed impatiently. "Gabriella. What are you talking about?"

"My dad once cared about me like that," she said. "My mom did, too. But no one since they died... no one has really..." To my shock, I heard a sniffle.

"Baby," I soothed, turning my head to the side. "Honey... are you crying?"

"Yessss," she moaned, full-on sobbing now. "I—you... you care about meeeee," she wailed.

Jesus Fucking Christ. Was she crazy?

"Of course I care about you," I gritted out. "Why else would I ask you to meet me? Why else would I get so worried that you weren't here when I asked?"

"That's my pooooinnnnttt," she wailed.

For Christ's sake. "Don't slacken your grip. Got it? Hold on, even if you're sobbing or whatever, okay?"

"Yes, Daddy," she whispered. "Okay, Daddy, I won't let go. I'll never let go. *Never!*"

I chuckled... I couldn't help it. I was pissed off and she *still* wasn't gonna sit for a week when I was done with her, but I couldn't stay mad. Not at Gabriella.

We rode in silence for a while until she spoke up from the back. "Dante? Where are we going? Do you know?"

"Yeah, baby," I said. "I know where we're going. Just trust me. I picked out a special place for us tonight."

She squealed then, legit, *squealed* like a little girl, and I laughed out loud.

"You are *too* good to me. Too, too good. Yayyyy! Oh, I can't wait."

"I'll get you back first thing in the morning, yeah?"

"Yes! *Yes!* Wooohooooo!" She yelled into the wind, and I kicked up the speed, dust flying behind me as we made our way to the place I'd selected. It was the most expensive place I could think of, but also the place that would really keep things quiet between us. I knew the owner, and our staying would be billed to a false account, with a fake I.D., and no one would be the wiser.

After half an hour riding, we made it. I did a quick spin around the parking lot to make sure we hadn't been followed. We were alone. For now, anyway.

I parked in the shadows at the back, where my friend had told me there were no cameras, and we could access the back door. He'd given me the security code and the number to the room, so we didn't even have to go up to the main desk but to the back. We walked past an elaborate swimming pool decked out with chairs, closed for now but lit with multi-colored lights. A large area outside the towering building housed a glowing fire pit and more chairs.

"Where are we going?" she whispered. "Oh, Dante. This is *amazing!*"

"Shh, Gabriella," I ordered, raising a finger to my lips. "This is our little secret, babe, so keep quiet, okay?" We hadn't even gotten to the good part.

She nodded and followed me as I input the codes and the door opened with a soft click. Thick, soft carpet welcomed us, glowing lights along the walls in elaborate sconces lending an air of luxury, refinement, and most importantly, privacy.

"Yes, Daddy," she whispered.

Once we'd made it to the top floor suite, she could make all the fucking noise she wanted, and that was my plan.

I hoped she'd make a *lot* of fucking noise.

We walked along the carpet that led to the elevator while she squealed about the thickness of the carpet, peeked into the enormous mirrors that hung on the walls, and held my hand with childlike wonder. I didn't burst her bubble until we made it to the elevator, and even then I only did it because I had other things on my mind.

"You're pretty excited for a little girl who's about to get a spanking," I said, leaning against the golden railing in the elevator and shaking my head. "Not sure you've fully understood my motives yet, Gabriella."

Her eyes widened and she stopped talking for a moment, looking around the interior of the elevator before speaking to me.

"And, um, what might those motives be?" she asked.

I leaned in, resting my forearm on the wall behind her, and placing my second hand on her hip as I stared into her eyes, pinning her in place. "To take you to a place where no one will hear you when you scream," I whispered. "To bring you to places you've never been, where you'll sing my name like a chorus until you're hoarse. To bring you mindless pleasure, baby. Again. And again. And again."

She blinked, breathing heavily, as the door to the elevator opened and I led her to our suite. I opened the door to our room, her eyes taking in everything around us in wide-eyed glee. She practically bounced on the pads of her feet, so excited about what was coming, and I hoped the suite I'd booked would please her. She deserved it.

The door opened and I held up a finger, wanting to go in ahead of her. I had to sweep the room. Always did.

"Oh, right," she whispered. "Gotta make sure there are no bad guys hiding in the corners, right?"

I rolled my eyes. After I'd convinced myself we were in the clear, I gestured for her to come in the room.

A bar ran along the edge of one wall, fully stocked and complete with bar stools, near a large window that overlooked the twinkling lights below us. With a tug of the shades we had privacy, though, and I smiled to myself. We'd need it.

The bed was absolutely gigantic, adorned with multiple pillows and blankets, in whites and golds, a full four-poster with filmy drapes that hung in ethereal swaths above. She'd feel like a princess.

"Wow," she said. "Just wow. This is... oh my goodness!" She squealed and when I turned to look at her, her arms were outstretched as she spun around the room in rapt fascination. This was mind-blowing to her and her delight in the little details of the room reminded me what it'd been like that first night we stayed together.

And that place didn't even hold a candle to this one. She was entranced, and I was smitten.

"This bathroom is totally bigger than my whole apartment," she said, running inside, her voice echoing in the large room. "I don't even know what all these knobs and buttons do. If you—oooh!"

I heard what sounded like a stream of water, and her little surprised reaction. Damn, she was so cute, and a little bit of a klutz.

"Gabriella," I said, shaking my head as I made it to the bathroom. "What the—"

But when I entered the room I got a full face full of water. I blinked, sputtering a bit, as I wiped my eyes with a wash-cloth she shoved in my hand.

"Oh my God, I am so sorry!" Her voice warbled, likely from the attempt at not laughing out loud. I shook my head as I finished wiping my face.

"What the hell?" I asked her, and she pointed to the jet trigger she held in her hand. "Gabriella," I said, trying to be patient but wanting to drag her out of the bathroom and make her behave herself. "Put that down."

She did, looking at me bashfully.

I crooked a finger at her. "Come here, please."

She walked over to me, biting her lip, and when she reached me, I yanked her close, wrapping one arm around her and tugging her so that she stood directly in front of me. I tapped her chin. "You like this place, don't you?"

"I do, Dante," she whispered. "This is... this makes me feel like a princess."

I held her close and kissed the top of her head.

"You're tired, baby. I can see it in your eyes, and the way your whole body leans up against me as if you just want to get some sleep."

She yawned, then, at the mere suggestion she was sleepy, and it reminded me of a little kitten waking up from a nap. I held her even tighter. "Do you just want to get some sleep?" I asked her. I'd let it go, all the plans I had for her, if she just needed some rest.

"Noooo," she said, laying her head against my chest. "I don't want to go to sleep now, Daddy. I want you to do… the things you said you would."

I held her close and lowered my hand to where her lower back sloped out to the fullness of her little ass. I squeezed.

"Oh yeah?"

"Daddy!"

"All the things I said I would?"

She tightened in my arms. "Wait. Wait just a minute. Does this mean that you're going to… you know?"

I felt my lips quirk. "Spank your ass?"

The breath left her in a whoosh. "Yeah."

"Of course."

"Oh, dear."

"Did you think 'oh dear' when you lied to me?" I asked sternly.

She shook her head and bit her lip.

I nodded slowly. Now that we were here and alone, I felt the rising need to touch her, to bring her close to me, to hold her and kiss her.

"Go, then," I said. "Go to the room and strip. When I come in, I want to see you kneeling by the side of the bed in nothing but your panties. Understand?"

Her mouth dropped open and she blinked.

I shook my head. "Not a very impressive attempt at obeying, little girl." She blinked again, and then she ran out of the room so fast I felt a little breeze pass me as she did.

I listened from the bathroom as I splashed some water on my face. She was quiet out there. I freshened up, and came to her a few minutes later. I wanted her waiting. Eager. Knowing she was about to be punished would put her in a good mindset, and I wanted to work that to my advantage.

She'd removed her clothes as I'd instructed, laying them neatly on the chair by a desk pushed up against the wall. She knelt by the side of the bed, wearing nothing but a thin pair of black satin panties. Her head was tilted to the side, and her cheek lay flat against the bed.

"Good girl," I said. "You did the right thing."

She turned to look at me and I quickly shook my head. No. I was in charge now. She'd obey.

"Turn back," I said sternly, swiveling a finger and pointing at the bed. She did as I commanded. "Good girl."

I watched her from where I stood, her thin, bare shoulders, the way the soft slope of her back gave way to the curves of her hips and backside, soft and creamy, the way she waited quietly for me as she knelt. Her nearly-white hair spilled on the bed, and one little hand was propped on the side of the bed while her other hand rested in her lap.

It was almost a shame I'd have to paint that creamy white ass red.

Almost.

I prowled up behind her and she did not move.

Good girl.

"Get up on the bed, Gabriella. Hands and knees," I instructed, giving her a second to process my instruction. After a brief second, she pushed herself up and got on the bed on all fours. "That's right," I said. "I want you holding onto the headboard while I punish you. You stay in position until I tell you to move. Yeah?"

"Yes, Daddy."

When she took her position, I stood behind her and slid down her panties. She shivered a little when she was bared, but like a good girl, stayed in position. I unfastened the buckle at my waist, and with a quick tug, pulled my thick leather belt into my hands. I folded it, and without a word snapped it against her ass, two quick stripes.

She gasped but held position.

"Good," I said, laying the belt down and walking to the large, overstuffed chair in the corner of the room while I admired the pretty pink stripes I'd laid across her ass. I watched her, kneeling on the bed naked now, a welt rising from where I'd spanked her with my belt. "Stay there a while, Gabriella," I commanded. "Think about how you're going to behave. And when I call you, come to me."

I watched as her chest heaved up and down, and she pulled her thighs together, her eyes shut tight. But she couldn't deny she was turned on. From where I sat, I watched as the glitter of arousal dampened her inner thighs.

The only sound in the room was her soft breathing, and the hum of the air conditioning in the background.

"Come here, now." She jumped, but she moved quickly to obey, releasing the bed rails and pushing herself off the bed. I watched her full, beautiful breasts bounce a little as she walked to me, her curvy hips swaying, still wearing the stripe from my belt as a badge of honor. I sat with my legs spread apart, still fully clothed, enjoying the power I held as she came before me naked, prepared to be punished.

Without a word, I pointed to the floor in front of me, and like a good girl, she knelt. Her gaze rested between my legs. I was painfully hard, and wanted nothing more than to feel her lips on me, to grab her soft blonde hair in my hands and twist, while I fucked her pretty little mouth.

As soon as she was close, I reached for her hair and threaded my fingers through it.

She smiled at me, silent. It was the quietest I'd ever seen her. Usually she had something she needed to talk about. But tonight, she was giving me the control.

I tipped a finger under her chin. "Will you behave your-self, baby?"

She nodded and looked away for a second before I tugged

her chin and brought her eyes back to mine. I leaned in, needing her to know that I was serious, even though I still wanted her aroused.

"Then lie over Daddy's lap."

CHAPTER TEN

 $\mathcal{I}$ stood, shaking a little, so turned on I thought I would die, but a little apprehensive as my belly hit his knee. He'd spanked me before, but this was different. Now, he was punishing me.

"You know how I felt when I realized you'd lied to me?" he asked. His deep, growly voice scraped over my skin as I wiggled over his lap, the rough feel of his jeans beneath my naked skin turning me on.

"No, Daddy. I didn't mean to lie." I protested, but the next second I yelped as his hand came down with a sharp crack on my bare backside. It hurt like crazy, and I got the message.

"I don't want an excuse," he said, with another sharp smack of his hand. "I want your obedience." He spanked me again, and my mind cleared. I couldn't think of anything as I laid there over his knee, and later, I realized I liked that. I could only think about how sexy he was and how I'd never lie to him again.

"A naughty girl who misleads her daddy needs a good,

hard spanking," he said, before unleashing another swift, painful torrent of smacks.

"Yes, Daddy!" I gasped.

"Good girl," he said, after another moment of steady spanks. He said nothing more as he continued to spank me. A sort of warmth flooded my core, and my ass was on fire, as arousal snaked its way through my whole body. My breath caught in my throat as my heart kicked up a steady beat, and I squirmed, needing more than the smack of his palm on my skin. I needed so, so much more.

His strong hand held my waist as his other hand dipped down to the curve of my ass. It stung, but as his palm smoothed over the heated skin, a warm, delicious thread of desire licked through me.

"Gonna be a good girl, Gabriella?" he whispered, massaging out the pain of my naked skin.

"Yes," I nodded. "Yes, Daddy." I could hardly speak I was so delirious with need, so desperate to feel release. "Daddy, please... please."

He rubbed my stinging backside again, then slowly pushed my legs apart.

"Please what?" he rasped, dragging a finger between my legs. "Fuck, baby, you're soaking for Daddy."

I squirmed and closed my eyes, but the truth was, he was right.

"Yes," I whimpered. He chuckled, but I didn't know what else to say. He'd punished me and I was going to fly right out of my skin.

"Open," he commanded in his deep rumble, pushing my legs apart. I obeyed on instinct, not knowing what he'd do but knowing I'd be okay with pretty much anything he wanted. My mouth opened as he pushed his fingers into my channel, then stroked over my clit. "Ah, good girl," he crooned. "Such a very good girl for Daddy, who's never gonna lie to him again. Right, good girl?"

"Nooo," I moaned. "Never. Oh my God, never ever again!"

I needed the release. My skin ached, my pussy throbbed, hot with need. He had to touch me.

"There you go," he said. "You're a lucky girl, Gabriella. I was gonna whip your ass with my belt, but I thought I'd take it easy on you," he whispered in my ear. I began to pant, my words becoming garbled. I was speaking nonsense, begging, pleading with him to put me out of my misery.

"There ya go," he murmured, picking me up and holding me in his arms.

"Daddy," I breathed, as he held me close to his chest, his erection pushed against my flaming hot backside.

"Listen to me, little girl," he said, as he stood with me in his arms as if I weighed nothing at all. "You listen to Daddy now. Are you listening?"

"Yessss."

"I want you to show me you trust me," he said. "Do you, baby?"

I nodded. He'd just spanked me and I wanted him to pleasure me and now he was looking at me like he had something else in mind instead of the orgasm I was dying for.

What was it?

He grinned darkly, flat out grinned, and I think it was the first time I'd ever seen his serious face break into a huge grin like that. "Listen, baby," he said. "I'm gonna lay you on that bed. I'm gonna take good care of you. But you'll come when I'm good and ready for you to come."

Whaaaat?

Was he... was he really doing that? For real? No way. No *way*. It was worse than being spanked. It was worse than being whipped with his belt.

Okay, who was I kidding? I freaking loved both of those things.

"Okay," I said, as he carried me to the bed and laid me down. "I trust you. I mean of course I trust you. Do you really think I'd have come with you all the way here if I didn't trust you?"

He grinned again and shook his head and muttered something about how cute I was.

I looked down bashfully when he chuckled, but then his eyes grew more serious and he pointed a finger at me. I took him in, then, in his worn jeans and t-shirt, so big and strong and stern. "Stay right there, baby," he said, looking around the room until his eyes rested on something in the distance. He narrowed his eyes, nodded his head, and walked to the dresser behind me.

The place was freaking huge, so when he walked away, I didn't know where he went or what he did. I just knew that he made me feel safe. He'd come for me and he cared about me. He'd beaten up the guys who were going to attack me the night before. And no, I didn't really know him all that well... yet... but there was something about the way he was with me that made me open my heart to him. Something that made me think, *yes, this, this is what I want. This is who I need.* So when he laid me on the bed and I felt my pulsing need, my backside aching from the strokes he'd given me, I knew.

I trusted him.

I started when I felt him right next to me at the head of the bed, but his eyes were focused elsewhere. "Stay still, Gabriella," he growled in my ear.

I was not going anywhere. Nope.

"Yes, Daddy." I nodded my head and closed my eyes, and seconds later something warm and soft touched my face. When I opened my eyes, though, I could see nothing.

I gasped. "Dante!"

"Right here, baby," in my ear. "Stay there, honey. Let yourself go. Can you let yourself go for Daddy?"

I swallowed and nodded. "Y-yes, Daddy," I said, though I felt my pulse quicken and my breath catch in my throat. "I'm here. I'm... I'm okay." But I wasn't okay. I was the little girl again, the one locked in a closet with lightning and thunder out the window, the little girl who needed a keeper, someone who cared about her.

Just minutes before, he'd spanked me for not telling me the truth. I could not lie to him now.

"No," I whispered, shaking my head from side to side, the cloth that covered my eyes dampening with sudden tears. "I-I can't lie to you. I told you I would tell you the truth. I-I'm scared being in the dark like this." And as soon as I spoke I felt his hand take mine, so strong, so warm.

"Daddy," I breathed, feeling the safety and security of the name, how sweet it was to call him that. "I—" My voice warbled and I felt him lift me and hold me up against him. Though I couldn't see a thing, I could feel him shift and hear the creak of the bed as he sat, cradling me in his arms. I could smell him, clean and strong and manly, and it warmed my belly.

His voice came to my ear, strong and secure. "Gabriella. You are safe here. No one is gonna hurt you. Face the fear. Ride it. Don't let it take you. Own it."

I swallowed hard and focused on holding his hand as he continued to coach me. "Breathe deep, honey. Big, deep breaths."

I already couldn't see anything, so I closed my eyes again, this time not trying to fight it, this time just listening to his voice.

He still held my hand, and he gave me a little squeeze.

"You're doing great," he told me. "Just like that now." His deep voice was almost melodic, now that the blindfold hid everything else, and all I could focus on now was the way he spoke, his rumbling voice soothing me, sending a wave of calm over me as he smoothed a hand through my hair. The feel of his fingers along my scalp pulled the tension out of my body, and between his voice and his calming touch, I released the tension. I inhaled deeply, feeling my entire body rise with the breath, then exhaled so slowly, bringing my body back down.

"What a good girl," he whispered in my ear. "This is about trust. You are strong, Gabriella. You can do this. And when you let things go and trust me, it means more to me than I can say. You aren't the little girl who's hurt, now," he said, his hand starting at my temples and slowly, softly, easing through my long hair, tugging along gently with a pull I felt through my whole body. "You're not the one neglected and hurt, baby. You're the one I'm going to ravish." He kissed my cheek, his warm body pressed up against mine as he whispered in my ear and held me. "Just trust."

I nodded. "I will," I said.

"Not gonna let you go," he promised. "The whole time, I'll touch you, so you can feel me."

His fingers left my hair and I felt his hand press against my shoulder, then both hands were encircling my waist. The bed shifted with his weight. I could see nothing through the blindfold, but soon my fears gave way to something far better, as the warm, sensual feel of his mouth lapped at my breasts. My breath came in gasps, and one of his hands grasped first one breast, then the other, kneading them as his tongue trailed along the sensitive skin.

"Good girl," he breathed, the warmth of his breath whispering along my skin. "That's Daddy's very good girl." His mouth was at my breast again, his tongue circling my nipple before he pulled it fully into his mouth and sucked, hard. My hips bucked and my hands flew up at the feel, but he was ready, his strong hands grasping my wrists and pinning them down.

"Feel," he commanded. "Just feel."

And so I did. The darkness swirling around me blocked out the noise in my mind, and a sort of quiet descended on me as he continued to lave my nipples, first one, then the other. His teeth grazed along the sensitive skin, a tingle of pain pierced my senses seconds before he asked forgiveness with the softest swipe of his tongue. One warm, strong hand kneaded my breast as the other made its way down my breastbone, past my belly, and lower still, to my pussy. The sensation of his mouth on my nipple while he teased me had me quaking beneath him, and every fear fled me as all I could do was lose myself to the sensuality, to my rising need, to the way he expertly manipulated my body.

His fingers explored my pussy, gently circling my clit, working me up as he stroked me. I was building, the sensations nearly overwhelming me. My ass still throbbed as he fondled me, and my need was rising with every stroke of his tongue against my nipple, every flick of his fingers on my clit. Without being able to see him, I didn't know what he'd do next. I was held somewhere between hope and ecstasy, needing him to take care of me. My breath caught in my throat as he lifted me again and laid me gently on the bed.

"Keep your hands there," he said, and I jumped a bit. His voice was back at my ear. A warmth covered my body as if he were laying atop me, but then I felt his mouth, first at my collarbone, then down to my breasts, teasing one nipple then the other, before tracing down to my navel. Both strong hands trailed down my sides as he lifted me, a flick of his tongue at the top of my thighs making me jerk with the sensation.

"Love that sweet pussy," he growled. "Daddy's gonna eat you out, baby."

I whimpered as he lifted my throbbing backside in his hands, and the next thing I knew, I was plunged into earth-shattering sensation as he took my pussy in his mouth, sucking my clit before releasing it and stroking upward, firm pressure that had me writhing on the bed. He worked me over, with soft, gentle caresses one second, flicks of his tongue the next, before he released me and sank his teeth gently into the sensitive skin at the top of my thighs.

"Oh, God," I moaned, unable to stop him, but I couldn't stand the sensation anymore. It was overwhelming me. I needed to climax *now*.

"Please," I begged. "Please, please, Daddy. Let me come. Please."

"Not yet," he growled, his rough voice almost angry before he rewarded my begging with another swipe across my swollen, throbbing pussy, his voice dropping lower still. "You come now and I'll spank you again. You disobey me now, and you won't sit for a fucking week. You come when I tell you and not a second earlier," he ordered.

"Dante," I moaned, pleading, begging, knowing I was gonna die if he didn't give me what I needed, and he froze.

Stopped.

He pulled his mouth off my pussy and held nothing but my hand.

"What did you call me?" he asked sharply.

"Dante," I said, recognition flooding me as I understood his anger. "I mean Daddy. Of course I meant Daddy! I'll call you anything you want, just let me come, Daddy!"

A deep, dark chuckle tickled my skin. "Baby," he said, his mouth at my ear. "You'll learn to trust Daddy. You do that by following my lead, yeah?"

I nodded with a wordless whimper, and his hands came to my sides again, before his tongue swirled a sensual circle along my lower abdomen and navel. "You do what you're told, or Daddy will have to punish you." I yelped as a sharp smack lit the top of my pussy on fire. He'd spanked me *there!* Then he squeezed my inner thigh, and flicked my breast. Each sensation built on the last as I wriggled beneath him and he delivered sharp smacks to my pussy and thighs between strokes of his tongue.

I couldn't hold off any longer. I was gonna come, and he would punish me. The very thought of being punished had me even closer to climaxing, but no, I didn't want to come, I couldn't not until he gave me permission.

"Are you gonna come for Daddy, Gabriella?" he asked with another upward stroke of his tongue that had me *right there*, right on the cusp, about to lose all control.

I nodded, while I blubbered and pleaded, no longer caring about being submerged in darkness, for all I could do was feel, my head tossing from side to side in near frenzy. "Please, Daddy."

"You'll be a good girl?" he rumbled in the darkness.

"Yessss," I promised.

His voice dropped. "Will you be my *bad* girl? Daddy's bad girl?"

"Yessss."

HIs guttural voice dragged across my naked skin like gravel. "Then ask for permission."

"May I, Daddy? May I come?"

His voice was like an answer to prayer, a benediction, as he whispered low, "Yeah, baby. Come for me." Another stroke of his tongue, and I was soaring.

I writhed beneath him, riding the waves of the most powerful climax I'd ever experienced, waves of ecstasy wracking my body. And I was still building, still climaxing as he expertly stroked me, holding me in his tight grip, my throbbing ass forgotten in the power of my climax. I could hardly breathe as he drained every last drop of pleasure from my body, and just as I thought I'd reached my peak, he plunged his fingers through my core and pumped, hard, and I climaxed again, the second orgasm more powerful than the first. I bucked beneath him, overcome with the mind-blowing sensations that seemed to go on forever, and finally, I floated back down to earth, exhausted.

I lay on the bed depleted, shattered, when I felt his warm body atop mine, his mouth at my ear. "Want to take that sweet pussy. Wanna feel you wrapped around my cock, baby."

"Yes," I breathed. It was the only thing I needed, the only thing that mattered.

I heard the crinkle of a wrapper and felt him shifting, and I knew he was putting on a condom. I felt his hard, hot cock at my entrance and to my surprise, a tug at the back of my head released my makeshift blindfold.

"Want you to watch me, baby," he said.

The blindfold fell to the side and I blinked, the only light in the room the dim illumination from the bathroom to the left. He grasped the edge of his shirt and took it off, whipping it to the floor, his muscles rippling.

Ho-ly shi-it.

I could see the rise of his broad back, his strong arms around me, the edges of his tattoos sneaking along his neck and shoulders. I shivered, still drunk from having climaxed so hard, completely at his mercy.

"Yes," I whispered, my arms encircling his neck. "Please, Dante. Yes, please,"

He grinned, his beautiful face lighting up, his eyes warming to me. "So beautiful," he said, briefly closing his eyes but opening them again as he nudged his cock in my entrance. I was so wet he slid in easily, and though I felt impossibly full, I felt little more than a mild ache.

"You okay, Gabriella? I'll be gentle this time."

This time. My pulse spiked at the thought of being taken hard and rough.

"Yes. Yes, please," I begged. And then he thrust, but I could tell he hesitated.

"I'm fine," I whispered. "Dante, do it. Don't hold back. Take me."

Perspiration dotted his forehead as he leaned down and touched his forehead to mine, moving in and out of me with controlled power. I felt so complete, so fulfilled, the discomfort mitigated by how right this felt. I could only sigh as he pumped in me again and again, until his own grunts met my ears as he squeezed me tight, his eyes rolling back as he came. A warmth spread across my chest as he lowered his body to mine, and our breath mingled in the darkened room.

I was his. His girl. Nothing in my life would ever be the same now. He'd made me his.

"Never knew what it would be like to take you," he whispered hoarsely, "Couldn't have predicted how it would feel." His head fell to my chest, and he lay there holding me.

"Did you like it? Did you, Dante? What you did to me was amazing and I never could have even imagined anything like it. Was it good for you, too, Daddy?" I needed to know.

He chuckled then, bringing his mouth to my forehead and kissing me with the ferocity that was all his. "Babe, *like* is an understatement. It wasn't good. It was fucking phenomenal. You gave me a gift, Gabriella. A precious gift, and I'll never forget that."

I smiled to myself and traced a finger along the tattoo on his shoulder.

"I'm glad," I whispered, knowing that what we had was special, and hoping that somehow, I could make this last.

CHAPTER ELEVEN

I stared at the girl beneath me, basking in the sweet flush of her cheeks, the way her eyes had fluttered closed as if she couldn't keep them open another minute. Her beautiful, full mouth smiled up at me as I rolled over to my side. I cleaned her up and tucked her under the covers.

I drew her onto my chest and smoothed a hand over her soft, silky hair, so blonde it was practically white, like a halo. She'd need a halo... the angel to my devil. The good girl whose wholesomeness warded off my sins.

When I first met her, I had this weird idea that she'd somehow redeem me, that just being near her I could erase the sins of my past. But now... looking at her, I knew that I would do anything to protect her, to keep her happy and safe, even if that meant selling my soul to do it. I'd lay down my life for this soft, sweet woman who gave it all to me. Her trust. Her blessing. Her love.

It didn't matter that we hadn't known each other for long. It didn't take long for someone to read goodness in another. It didn't take long to know that she was meant for me, but how could she be mine? How would I keep her safe? For the moment, I had to push aside the doubts that tormented me and enjoy what I had right here, right now.

And as I held her against me in the dark quiet of the room, she moved a bit closer, pressing her luscious, naked body up against mine. "You're so strong," she whispered, tracing a finger along the muscles of my shoulders and arms. "How did I get to be taken care of by a big, strong, guy like you? I thought I'd only... I dunno, date dweebs or something."

I chuckled. "You're friggin' adorable, you know that?"

"What?" she asked, smiling up at me. "I'm just telling you the truth. I thought I'd end up with like... a banker or something. A guy that wore sweater vests and boat shoes and talked about his mutual funds. Or a regular old guy who was sweet and kind and a hard worker, but who never really rocked my world. I just... never in my wildest dreams could I imagine being with a man like you. A guy who's so dominant and sexy, and... I had no clue it would be so hot to be spanked," she said with a shrug. "Or blindfolded. And now I'm thinking, heck, maybe if you're up for it we can even maybe go to like one of those BDSM clubs? You know? Where you can tie me up or something?"

I laughed out loud, the sound startling her as she jumped a bit.

"What's so funny?" she whispered. "I wasn't joking. I'm serious!"

"That's what's so funny, baby," I answered. "I know you're serious. And the truth is, I don't know how we found each other. But I enjoy the hell out of you. I want to take care of you. And, I will. But no fucking way am I taking you to a place where anyone else will lay eyes on you but me."

"Come here," I said, pulling her tighter and kissing her forehead.

She giggled. "Your whiskers tickle, Daddy."

"It's late, baby. We need some rest. And tomorrow, I want to give you a good breakfast before you go home."

I wanted to take care of her. I knew she needed more than she got. I knew she was poor, that much I could tell, from the way her clothes were faded and worn, her cell phone was outdated, her body a little thinner than it should have been. Though she was my beautiful girl, she needed a keeper.

I'd be that keeper.

"Beautiful little girl," I said, not able to stop myself from worshipping her as she lay in my arms, her soft, trusting body pressed up against mine. "Beautiful, sweet girl."

She smiled, and her eyes began to close.

"You're so tired, babe. Get some sleep now."

"I don't want to go to sleep," she said. "If I go to sleep, I'll wake up and it'll be time to go home and then I have to say goodbye. Can't I just stay awake?" she asked, even as her eyes drooped closed.

"No, Gabriella. Sleep now. Rest your eyes. We'll find a way that we can still be together. Got it?"

She nodded, and then she was breathing deeply, her chest rising and falling as she welcomed slumber. I reached down and pulled up the edge of the blanket, covering her as she slept. I held her like that, up against my chest.

Sweet, sweet girl.

I lay in the darkness until I grew sleepy myself, but I couldn't shut off my mind. My worries and fears went on and on, plaguing me.

What if my father found out who she was? Emilio? What would they do to her? How would I protect her?

What if she found out who I was?

All these questions and more kept me awake long after she'd fallen asleep until finally, I pushed myself out of bed. I padded around the room and grabbed a bottle of water from the little refrigerator at the bar. Twisting the top, I gulped in large, cold sips of water, draining the bottle. I tossed it into the trash, and walked to the window, flicking a curtain to the side.

Son of a bitch.

A gleaming black SUV sat right under our window.

I'd recognize that car anywhere. From where I stood, I could see only one thing, but it was enough: the driver had one long, silver scar that ran across his jaw. Even though he sat in the shadows, I knew that scar ran to his hairline, a souvenir from the first day he'd fought for the honor of the family and put a man in the grave.

Emilio. Of all the godforsaken people...

It was a big fucking deal to be the one who inherited the family, the one who stepped up as leader of the most well-respected organized crime networks in all of Vegas. So much so that he had to hunt me down, had to spy on me? I clenched the drapes in my fists and watched as he started the car and pulled away. He knew, and that was all he needed. I stalked back to the bed where she lay, her arm over her forehead like a child who'd fallen asleep after a long day at an amusement park.

My anger ebbing, I sat on the edge of the bed. Just the sight of her calmed me. I'd worn her out.

I climbed in beside her, lifting the sheets and blankets up over my shoulders. She rolled toward me in her sleep, and I pulled her close, spooning her from behind. As I wrapped my arm around her small, slumbering frame, her presence seeped through me like a drug, relaxing me. I nestled my flank against her soft, curvy ass and my face against her hair, inhaling deeply, as if breathing her in would cleanse me. I closed my eyes and sighed.

She made me want to be a good man.

And lying next to her, I forgot about the man who lay hidden in the darkness outside my window.

Fuck the family. I had all I needed right here. Tomorrow, when the sun rose, I would make this right... somehow. I had to.

"*W*ake up, Daddy." I felt a sharp tug on my beard, and her scent enveloped me.

"Hey," I said, my voice still husky from sleep, as I opened one eye and found Gabriella laying on my chest, twirling my beard in her fingers, looking up at me with those huge, beautiful eyes.

"Finally!" she said, her whole face lighting up with a smile. "I thought you were like *never* gonna wake up. I've been trying to get you to open your eyes and you kept growling and grunting."

I opened the other eye and couldn't help but smile at her. "You know, there are better ways to wake a man up than to pull his beard." With a quick tug, I had her flat over my chest, so that her body was pressed up against me, my dick already hard against her soft belly.

She bit her lip and grinned, her eyes warming as my hands traveled down the length of her beautiful body and cupped her ass.

"You awake now, Dante?" she asked, brows raised hopefully.

I lifted her and turned so that I lay above her, pinning her beneath me.

"You could say that," I rasped in her ear, grinding my erection against her naked leg. Fuck, yeah. "You've been a naughty girl, waking up Daddy."

"Oooh," she said with a teasing glint in her eyes, her voice dropping to just above a whisper. "Maybe Daddy needs to punish me then. Punish me by..." Her voice lowered so much

I could hardly hear her, as her cheeks flushed pink and she licked her lips... "Fucking me hard."

Jesus Christ.

"On your chest," I rumbled against the shell of her ear. With an adorable squeal, she wiggled out from under me, flipped onto her belly, got up on all fours and arched her back.

Oh, *hell yeah.*

I slapped her bare ass with the flat of my palm so hard she jerked forward, then slid right back into position with a whimper, wriggling her ass for more. I slapped just below the curve of her ass, at the tender spot where her thighs met her backside, leaving a pink handprint before I rubbed the sting away. Her thighs glistened with arousal, and I gave her another sharp smack, then another, each slap making her huff out a breath.

I leaned against her, my cock pressed to her ass, and wound my fingers around her soft blonde hair before I gave it a sharp tug. Her mouth fell open just before I leaned down and licked her neck, suckling the sweet skin into my mouth before I bit down, just enough to make her pant, but not enough to leave more than a slight mark.

"Oh my God," she breathed.

I pushed her face down against the pillows, cheek flat against the white pillowcase, and whispered in her ear.

"You stay right here while Daddy takes what's his. I wanna fuck your sweet pussy again, Gabriella. Yeah?"

She nodded her head so hard and fast I thought she'd give herself whiplash. "Yes, Daddy."

"Stay. *Right. There,*" I ordered as I stripped out of my boxers. She whimpered but obeyed, and I took a moment to appreciate the vivid perfection of her submission to me, her chest on the bed, beautiful eyes closed in trust, ass painted red from my hand. She took what I gave her and asked for more.

"I wanna take you, Gabriella, and I wanna take you hard but you tell me if it's too much."

"It's not too much."

I chuckled. "Haven't done it yet, babe."

I took her hips and held them before I ground into her sweet, wet pussy, holding her tight so she could feel how much I wanted her, but careful not to hurt her. She pushed right back against me, though, inviting harder.

So damned perfect.

I fucked her like I meant it, like this was the last time we'd have this perfection, and she took every stroke.

"God, yes. Just like that. Oh my God, that's so good, Dante."

Fuck yes.

With a final thrust of my hips, she came, her head thrown back as she screamed my name, and I followed her, chasing my own ecstasy, needing this, needing to fucking own her.

I held her tight against me.

"Jesus, baby. I didn't think you could take that."

She giggled, eyes shut tight with her head still up against the pillow. "I think I'm drunk. I'm... sex drunk. Wow. Just..." She sighed a happy sigh.

I chuckled. "Worked up an appetite?"

She shrugged. "I didn't have much to eat yesterday. So I'm starving."

I didn't like that she didn't get enough to eat, or that she had a shit phone, and that her needs were likely not met.

I would change that.

"Let's fix that," I said, as I tossed her down on the bed and swung my legs over the side. I nabbed the menu. "You like eggs?" She nodded her head. "French toast?" Her eyes grew wide and she smiled.

"I love French toast."

"Bacon? Toast?"

"Yes, and yes."

I chuckled. "Baby, is there anything you don't like?"

"For breakfast?" she asked, and I nodded.

"Um. Cream of wheat. Nasty sludge. Oatmeal is also most disgusting, as are frosted flakes." She shuddered.

I grinned, picked up the phone, and tried to place the order.

"I'm sorry, sir," came the voice on the other end of the line. "We aren't open for room service for another hour."

"What if I pay you for it?" I asked, lowering my voice and turning my back to her so she couldn't overhear. A few hundred dollars later, the food was on the way.

"Dante," Gabriella said, her scolding. "What did you just do?"

I hung up the phone and shrugged. "What?"

"Did you just bribe someone?" she raised a brow at me, like a stern mama. It was fucking endearing, and not at all intimidating.

"Nope," I said, pulling her onto my lap and kissing her cheek.

"Don't distract me, Dante," she said, wagging her finger at me.

"Not distracting you," I said, my mouth at her collarbone now, dragging my tongue along the sensitive skin, grinning as her breathing grew labored.

"Listen... to... me," she puffed out, as I sucked her sweet skin into my mouth. She wiggled a little.

"I did not bribe, babe," I rumbled in her ear. "I paid someone to go above and beyond the call of duty. It's different."

She raised a brow. "In-indeed."

"Now, now, baby. You listen to me. C'mere," I said, kissing

the apple of her cheek before I whispered in her ear. "I did nothing wrong here." If she even fucking knew the things I'd done...

"Baby, who's the daddy here?"

She wiggled on my lap a bit and my cock lengthened beneath her ass. Jesus, my need for her was insatiable. "You," she said. "But I am just—"

I held her in one hand while I tipped her up and smacked her ass with the other. "This conversation is over."

"Fine," she huffed.

"Gabriella," I warned, as she peeked up at me from beneath lowered lashes. I grinned, pinned her down, and rolled her over so that she was on top of me.

"Now I'm on top," she teased. Ten minutes later, I'd shown her exactly how she *wasn't* in charge and left her breathless and grinning when a knock came at the door. I set her on her feet and pointed for her to stay right where she was.

I looked through the peephole, my senses on high alert, not sure what to expect. Emilio with a tray of breakfast foods?

But no, a gangly, teenaged kid in a burgundy suit coat stood in front of the door with a tray of food. I opened the door, and when he saw me, he blinked.

Shit. I forgot that many recognized me, fake name be damned. The kid shook like a fucking leaf.

"Your food, sir," he said in an unnaturally high squeak. I wanted to tell him to grow a pair, but instead I slapped the cash in his palm, thanked him, and balanced the tray in my hand, shutting the door behind me before hitting the dead-bolt and sliding the security chain in place.

"Oh my God, are we feeding a small third world country?" Gabriella asked, staring. She'd moved to the table that stood by the window, her slender leg tucked under her ass.

I grinned and lifted lid after lid, the room filling with the scents of coffee, bacon, and cinnamon. My stomach growled.

"I worked up at appetite with all the activity last night," I said with a shrug.

"Dante!"

I grinned, flicked open a white napkin, and nestled it over her lap. "Yeah?"

"You just..." and then she shook her head. "Yeah. It was so... *hot*. I'm starving, too."

Chuckling, I slid a plate of food over to her and opened the lid of her hot chocolate. I blew on it a little, cooling it for her, before I handed it to her. I sat down and got down to business myself.

"When you're done, gotta get you home. Restaurant opens in what, an hour?"

She nodded glumly. "Yeah. My stepmother has gone strangely quiet," she said. "Like, I would expect her to be all up in my business, trying to see where I was, but she's backed off." She shrugged a shoulder. "Don't question a good thing, I guess, huh?"

No. You had to fucking question everything. The skin prickled at the back of my neck. You didn't run the show as son to Antonio Villanova without developing strong goddamn senses, and mine were telling me something was wrong.

I didn't want to send her back.

"Can you tell her you can't work today? You're sick or something?"

She paused, a forkful of eggs halfway to her mouth. "You mean lie?"

God, her moral code was adorable.

I shook my head. "I don't know. Something isn't right. Something has me concerned is all, and I want to keep you safe."

She put her fork down as her eyes gentled. "That's sweet. But I'm not sure what you mean, or how you would."

I bit angrily into a piece of toast, quietly mulling my options. She had a point. Where would I keep her? Short of making her mine and flying to a foreign country and changing my identity, how *could* I truly keep her safe? It wasn't possible.

"Eat your breakfast," I ordered, more gruffly than I really needed to. "We need to go."

She nodded. "I had a fantastic night, Dante," she said quietly, laying her hands in her lap.

"Me, too, Gabriella." The words seemed strangely suspended, like it was the last time we'd be together like this. "Babe, I need to ask you something."

She swallowed, dabbed her pretty lips daintily with a napkin, and nodded. "Yes, Daddy?"

"Your whole name, Gabriella. Where you live. Where you work. I want the truth."

Her green eyes met mine in challenge. "Will you tell me yours?"

I sucked in a breath, then exhaled sharply. "No."

Tipping her head to the side, I watched as her eyes grew guarded. How could I expect her to tell me the truth of her identity when I wouldn't do the same?

"My name is Gabriella Madison."

Her last name was vaguely familiar.

I hated that it was. Ignorance would have been so much better.

"Pleased to meet you, Gabriella Madison." I reached for her hand. "And I know that you didn't want me to know all that, but I'm honored you confided in me."

She smiled. "I feel lighter, having told you," she confessed. "Freer."

I didn't care who she was, if she lived in a hovel in the

corner of the street. All that mattered was that she was mine. That she trusted me. I took her hand and kissed her fingers.

Today, she had to work, and I had to prepare for the big fucking masquerade ball. It was time to leave.

"Let's finish up and get going," I whispered.

She smiled softly at me. "Yes, Daddy."

When we were done eating, we got dressed, and it took all the willpower I had not to lay her on the bed, strip her bare, and ravish her once more. But we didn't have the time.

And I wouldn't rush it.

"Let's go, baby," I said, my voice husky, as I sat beside her. I pulled her to standing and pushed my chair out so that I could draw her between my knees.

"Oh my God, I am so full," she moaned, standing in front of me, placing her hands on my shoulders while I kissed the soft skin at her neck. Her breaths shortened but she continued. "That was so yummy though. I love when they make French toast crispy but soft and the bacon all crunchy and the syrup was still warm. Mmmm. Daddyyyyy."

My tongue grazed along her neck.

"It was good," I rasped. "You taste better."

She hugged me, her hardened nipples scraping along my bare chest, and my cock strained for release. I wanted to fuck her so badly.

"We have to go," she whispered, wrapping her hands around my shoulders and lowering her head.

"I know." I pulled her so hard the small of her back was flush against me as I took her mouth in a hard, claiming kiss that made her head go back and her knees tremble as I held her, letting her feel my strength, a kiss she would not forget. Finally, though it half fucking killed me, I released her.

"Let's go," I growled. "Let's get you home."

She rested her forehead against mine briefly, the breath of a touch we both knew underscored the sheer reluctance.

I'd tasted goodness and I wanted more. So. Much. More. I wanted normal. When I cradled Gabriella in my arms, the blood-stained hands that held her were washed clean. The sins of my past forgotten.

We packed our things in silence, and she held my hand as I opened the door. I scanned the hall, not much caring who I walked into. I'd had my night with her. And now I had to find the strength to let her go.

I had choices to make. Choices that would fucking kill me.

She couldn't follow me into the darkness.

CHAPTER TWELVE

*T*he ride back to town wasn't as fun as the ride out. Dante had grown strangely quiet and broody, and when I tried to talk to him he didn't say much.

"Are we meeting tonight?" I asked. It had almost become our thing already, our midnight rendezvous.

"I can't tonight, babe," he said, as he pulled onto the busy freeway and I held on tighter, the bike kicking up and humming beneath me.

"Why can't you?"

"I have somewhere to be that I can't get out of. Believe me," he yelled over his shoulder, his words dying in the wind. "If I could, I would. I've got a big fucking party for my family."

A party?

I squirmed behind him, turned on already. He'd played me over and over the night before, and now my body was primed for him, the sound of his voice making my insides quiver. My clit throbbed with the hum of the bike.

There were far better things we could've been doing. I

shook my head, and swallowed, trying to be a good girl. But being around him made it pretty difficult to do.

My throat tightened a bit. I wanted to see him. "When will I see you again?"

"Tomorrow night? Can you do that? Meet me?"

"Of course I can," I said. I would do anything I had to. I *needed* to see him again like my life depended on it.

As we pulled up to the place where he always left me off, a strange sense of foreboding wove its way into my belly. I wouldn't see him tonight, and tomorrow seemed so far away now. And if I went that long without seeing him, it seemed as if anything could happen. Anything could pull us apart.

He held the bike steady for me as I swung my legs off and took my bag across my back.

"Thank you for breakfast," I whispered. "Thank you for everything."

He looped a hand around my neck and pulled me to him, brushing my forehead with his warm lips. "You're welcome, baby. I'll miss you. Be good, and don't forget to meet me tomorrow at midnight. Yeah?"

"Okay," I whispered. So many words hung in the air between us, so many things left unsaid. We couldn't go on like this, clandestine meetings at midnight, never getting to the point where he met my family or I met his. Never accepting that this was a reality we couldn't change.

"Be good, Gabriella," he said, releasing me and sending me off with a sharp crack to my ass.

Yikes. As if I needed him to stoke my arousal.

I walked away, him at my back, feeling his eyes on me the entire time.

Something was wrong. I paused and looked back at him, but he looked the same, sexy as hell, leaning against his bike with one foot propped up, his huge arms crossed over his chest as his stern eyes met mine. He gave me one nod and a chin lift.

Go.

But as I left, something told me that things were never going to be the same again.

"Ooooh," Violet said, as I wiped down the tables in the very back row of La Bistro. "I feel like... like a princess!" From where I stood, I could see the office piled high with boxes. A little pang of jealousy wove through me.

I wanted pretty things, too.

"Gabriella! Gabriella, come here!" With a sigh, I put my rag down, washed my hands, and made my way to where Dress Fest was going on. Elenora stood in the corner, surrounded by pretty pink tulle, piles of tiaras, boxes of shoes, and a plethora of beautiful dresses. Agatha must've maxed out her credit card for this splurge, but she'd likely return most of it.

"What do you think?" Violet stood in front of me, her hands on her hips, dressed in a shiny green dress. She looked... interesting. Like a dressed up dragon or something.

"That's a very pretty dress," I said as politely as I could.

"You look like a stuffed olive." Agatha's terse voice traveled from behind the boxes. I hadn't heard her come in. "Not the one for you. Pick another," she snapped, waving her hand toward the pile of dresses.

Elenora stepped in then, dressed in an intricate, sleeveless crimson gown with gold accents and a vee that dipped so low in the front you could practically see her navel. "And this?" Elenora asked, spinning around in a floor length gown fit for a princess.

"Oh, you look beautiful," Agatha said.

And she really did look stunning, gold platform heels below the dark red hem dramatically elevating her height.

"Get another dress on, Violet," Agatha ordered.

My stepmother's gaze met mine across the room. "Why are you here?" she snapped. "Shouldn't you be serving customers?"

I sighed. At least the old Agatha was back. The old Agatha was predictable. I'd asked her about the night before, and she'd feigned total innocence so convincingly, I felt as if I'd dreamed the whole thing up.

"Yeah," I said. "Thanks for the reminder. Later, girls."

Silence met my proclamation as I walked out of the office and back to where I was cleaning. And then it hit me.

I was so stupid. So naïve. The party that Dante was going to... Could it be the same one?

"Hey." I looked up to see Ruby waiting for me at her regular table. "You look both exhausted and pissed. What's going on?"

I shook my head. "I was up late last night is all, and I'm exhausted and mostly fed up with talk about this party. Gold this and necklace this and shoes that." I plunked down in a chair across from Ruby, hoping Agatha would be occupied enough that she wouldn't come in and see me sitting down on the job. "And I just had a horrible, terrible thought that the party *my* guy is going to is the one *they're* going to, and I'm not."

She shook her head. "You are the one who *should* be going to this," she said in an exasperated tone. "You're the beautiful, deserving one who doesn't get opportunities like this."

"But I'm not the *elite*," I grumbled. "Remember?"

Ruby frowned, and I stood to go. "I wish I could go, Ruby. But I see no possible way."

"Doesn't matter," she said. "Where there's a will, there's a way. You have to work tonight?"

I nodded. "Yeah."

"Let me help, Gabriella."

I shook my head. "No, I'm all set, really."

"Gabriella!" Now it was Elenora calling me. I sighed and shook my head at Ruby.

"You're sweet, Ruby, but we have to be practical." I headed back to the office, and this time Elenora was sitting with her hair piled on her head, long, glittery earrings dangling from her ears, wearing a hideous, tight-fitting sequined number.

"What about this one?"

"It's lovely. I think they both are, to be honest with you."

"I think I know what I'll wear then!"

I'd always been nice to my step-sisters, even if they were nasty to me. But now... now the thought of Dante showing up and being anywhere near either one of them sickened me. How would I know if it was really the place he was going, though? Surely there were hundreds of parties in Vegas tonight? And I had so much to do...

As the day wore on, however, it seemed my tasks were monumental, and for a brief moment I considered saying screw it. Disappearing. Going... somewhere else.

Finding Dante.

I so wanted to live my own life, to leave the grueling work at the restaurant and my stepmother's non-stop demands behind. But then I'd hear my father's voice again, asking me to take care of her.

I had given him my word, and I'd loved my father. Breaking a promise to him would destroy me. As I carried a load of dirty dishes to the back, stacking them up to be cleaned, I made myself remember what it was like, being a little girl without a care in the world.

And I realized then, as the weight of my responsibilities

consumed me, that I still felt that way. Even now, as an adult... being with Dante made me feel that way again.

And I wanted him, now. I wanted to feel his strong arms around me, telling me everything would be okay, that he was proud of me, that I was his special girl. I sighed as a wave of longing washed through me. And, in return, I wanted to make him smile... wanted to make those gorgeous eyes light up with happiness just from the silly little things I said without even meaning to. I never meant to make him laugh, I just spoke whatever I thought. But he liked that I did.

I wanted him to lay me down, and do the deep, dark, deliciously sexy things he did, playing my body bit by bit, taking me to heights I'd never been. I'd be his good little girl.

I smiled to myself. I'd be his bad little girl, too.

I never heard her come in the room, but when she spoke I nearly jumped out of my skin.

"What are you smiling about?" Agatha sneered, crossing her arms and staring at me. "You seem like you have a little secret that's just yours, and yet you haven't told me anything."

"Oh, nothing." She would not taint this.

"Nothing?" she asked, head cocked to the side. "If you say so. Truthfully, I think you're lying but I have neither the time nor the inclination to pursue this."

A cold feeling of dread crept along my spine.

Maybe I didn't owe it to my father to take care of her. It seemed Agatha was perfectly fine taking care of herself.

"Nothing to worry about," I reiterated with forced nonchalance. "Really. Did you sort out the clothing for Violet and Elenora?"

She shrugged, still eyeing me, her arms stretched over her chest. "We're getting there. Don't forget to prepare the marinade for tomorrow, and to be sure the new seasonal menus are pulled out. Table the old ones, and mark off what we need to order." She continued with a litany of things she needed done, *tonight,* before she pushed herself off of the counter she leaned against and stalked off. I went back to my tasks. The food from breakfast still kept me full enough that I could skip lunch, and maybe, if I finished everything... maybe I'd find a way I could go tonight.

I glanced at the clock and swiped a hand across my sweaty brow. I shook my head. I wanted to see Dante, and tonight I would see my sisters dressed up and going to the masquerade ball that dreams were made of. I looked at the list of things I still had to do, and I shook my head. There was no way this was going to work. No way I'd finish everything I needed to do, and I wasn't quite sure I wanted to. After another hour of working, I finally sat on a bench, my shoulders sagging.

I'd never be done in time. And what if I miraculously made it, only to find out that it wasn't what I'd thought it was at all? That he wasn't even there?

"Gabriella?" I looked over my shoulder and blinked. Ruby stood in the doorway to the kitchen, and she looked oddly gleeful.

"Why do you look so happy?" I asked her. "What's going on?"

"Oh, nothing," she said, then she clapped her hands like a little girl.

"Nothing?" I pushed myself to my feet and stared at her, putting my hands on my hips. "Ruuubby. What are you hiding?"

"Gabriella," she said, crossing into the kitchen which was technically against the policy, but I didn't much care, as Agatha and the girls had long since left to get their hair and nails and makeup done.

"You're going to that party tonight."

I blinked. "What? How? Why would I do that?" But even as I questioned her, hope rose in my chest.

She leaned in and hissed in my ear. "Because he'll be there."

A warmth spread across my cheeks as I pulled away. "Who, Ruby?"

She shook her head and rolled her eyes heavenward. "For God's sake, honey. *Dante, of course!* I'm a millionaire several times over. You don't think I have a vested interest in the man that makes you light up like a firecracker? Hmm? You don't think that I want to see you happy? So maybe I dug around a little."

My throat felt strangely clogged, my eyes damp with tears. I didn't know what to say, so I said the only thing I could. "Thank you."

She reached out and pulled me to her, holding me in a fierce embrace before releasing me. "Darlin', you listen to me. He has a ball to go to tonight. And *you're* going to be there with him."

I shook my head. "How, Ruby? Look at this list of things I need to do before I can go. If I don't, she'll fire me, and then what will I do? She'll make my life a living hell!"

Ruby nodded, then stepped back and snapped her fingers. "Come in!" My mouth dropped open in shock as a team of men and women in uniform marched in.

"I need to do this for you," she said. "You were the one who listened when my husband passed away. You've been the only one who has been there for me, day in and day out, when no one else seemed to care. What am I going to do with all this time and money I have anyway? I can't take it with me." She shook her head. "This team will do what needs to be done here. You, you're coming with me, kiddo. First, tell them what to do." I blinked and looked around. I had a full dozen people waiting for my command. Within minutes, all jobs were delegated, and I turned to Ruby, excitement building in my chest, hope rising.

She reached for my hand and yanked me, bringing me along with her. I followed in a sort of stupor, not knowing where we were going or what would happen. This was all surreal.

I had to get there. I couldn't *not* be there.

"Ruby. I have only one problem here, and it's a pretty, like, major problem."

"Nah," she said, pulling me down the length of the street and to the open door of the upscale complex where she lived. She ushered me past the doorman and shoved me in an elevator, clapping her hands while her eyes danced. "This will be so fun," she whispered. "Just call me your fairy godmother."

Laughter, borne of nerves and excitement, bubbled up inside me. "Ruby!" I could only shake my head.

"So what's this problem?" she asked, raising a brow.

I shook my head and gestured at the work jeans, faded top, and scuffed flats I wore. "I can't wear this to a masquerade! Honestly, Ruby, it wouldn't be right. And I have no time or money to do anything about that."

She pursed her lips and placed a well-manicured hand with pointy red nails on her hip, while wagging a matching red-tipped nail at me. "What did I just tell you?" she chided. "*I'm your fairy godmother.*"

"And what exactly does this mean?"

She merely giggled to herself like a little girl. "You're gonna see exactly what I mean in a few minutes."

So her "sources" said that Dante would be at the party. Alrighty then. So would Agatha, and her daughters. The very thought of any of them being anywhere near him...

"I'll bitch slap them," I hissed before I even realized what I was saying. My hand flew to cover my mouth.

Had I just said that out loud?

Ruby reared her head back and stared. "What?"

"Oh my God. I was just... thinking. That I could go. But

then I remembered that Agatha and her daughters were going to be there, and the idea of either one of them being anywhere near Dante... I just." I shook my head as our elevator cruised to a stop at Ruby's floor. "I've never been one for violence, Ruby. It's astonishing to me that the words just tumbled out of my mouth like that."

Her mouth hung open as the door to the elevator opened, before she burst into laughter. Her peals of laughter rang through the hallway and she had to grip the walls for support. "You—you're just—you're this tiny, sweet little thing, but suddenly, the thought of your sisters... Oh, this is perfect. We *have* to get you there!" She wiped her eyes and blew her nose into a tissue while I watched in a sort of half-amused, half-embarrassed stupor. "Come with me," she said, pulling me along once again. "You haven't been to my place in ages."

I hadn't. I used to drink tea with her up in her penthouse, and she'd tell me about her husband and feed her crazy little poodle expensive treats that smelled like bacon, and we'd talk about my father and my mother. But Agatha grew jealous, and she'd give me job after job to do. It seemed my free time had ended. I hadn't been to Ruby's in months, if not longer.

"Tonight, it'll be like old times. Except with fancy dresses. And a lover who's pining away for you." Her voice got all choked up and I thought she was going to cry, but when I looked at her with concern, she burst out laughing. "And bitch slaps." She slapped her thigh so loudly the sound echoed in the hallway.

"Ruby!" I hissed. "Compose yourself. And stop making fun of me!"

"Oh, honey, I'm not making fun of you," she said, as she opened the door to her penthouse. She sobered as she stood and looked at me before we went in. "I couldn't be prouder. You have no idea, Gabriella, how badly I want to see you happy." My throat tightened but there was no more time to chat, as she yanked me into her house. "But enough about that. Time to ditch those duds, kiddo. You're moving on up."

She gestured for me to follow her, and when I stepped into her apartment, I blinked in surprise. Her place had always been incredibly opulent. Crystal chandeliers decorated the dining room, the walls were adorned with paintings she'd acquired from across the world, and I stepped on a vibrantly-colored, hand-woven Oriental rug. But what held me in rapt fascination was what stood in her living room: an array of ball gowns, and jewelry and attendants waiting for me, one with a large mirror and palette of cosmetics, one with a measuring tape, and still more at the ready.

"Off to the powder room first," Ruby announced merrily. "Time to pretty up your hair!" I followed her in a daze, shaking my head at the wonder of it all. "Just let me do this for you," she whispered in my ear, before she handed me over to her stylist. "And when we are done, we'll deliver you to your man. Got it?"

I shivered. *My man.*

I swallowed, straightened my shoulders, and walked with purpose toward the woman who waited for me.

Dante was waiting. And I had a job to do.

*A*n hour later, I stepped in front of the mirror and sighed in amazement. I wore a tight-fitting baby blue gown with silver accents that made me feel like a fairy princess. It glimmered and shone but dipped dangerously in the front, revealing more cleavage than I'd anticipated. I didn't even know I *had* that much cleavage. Diamonds twinkled at my neck, with matching glittering diamonds in my ears. My hair was piled on my head in loops and swirls, and I wore a matching diamond tiara on my head. My make-up brought out the green in my eyes, my lashes so long I blinked in shock. My cheeks were the faintest pink, my lips a rosy gloss several shades deeper. I turned my head and glanced from side to side, hardly recognizing the reflection that stared back at me before I brought the handheld mask I was supposed to wear to my face.

"You look *exquisite,"* Ruby breathed.

"I look... different."

She shook her head. "Good. That's the point. You *should!"*

"No one will recognize me."

"Perfect!"

Laughter bubbled up inside me then, and I grinned at her. "Okay. Let's do this." I lifted my dress and pointed a bare foot. "So when do I get my glass slippers?"

She grinned and snapped her fingers, and a woman came bustling in with shoes on a *tray,* like they were petit fours at high tea.

"Not gonna eat them," I muttered to Ruby, who only laughed and playfully smacked my hand.

"Choose your favorite," she said. "They're customized just for you. And when you're ready, off you go."

"Customized? How does that work?"

She shrugged. "One of a kind. You wear them, and Belinda makes them match your dress, your eyes, your toes, I dunno. She just makes it perfect."

I looked at her in disbelief. *"Really?"*

She nodded. "Really. Do it, Gabriella."

Thirty minutes later, I walked to the limo that awaited. I felt as if I floated. My gown billowed out around me like a cloud. The gorgeous slippers Belinda had fashioned clinked as I walked, and I held a clutch in my hand that felt as if it were accented with real silver and gems.

I'll blink any minute, and wake up, and realize this had all been a dream.

"He's waiting, Gabriella. *Go,*" Ruby whispered. "And tomorrow, you'll tell me all about it."

"I will," I promised, reaching out to Ruby and hugging her. "*Thank you.*"

She waved her hand at me, and off we went into the night. I had no idea how this would play out—whether he'd recognize me in my mask, whether he'd be happy to see me when he did. All I knew was that fate had led me to this place, and I didn't want to spend another midnight without my prince.

CHAPTER THIRTEEN

" *L* ooks fine," I said, nodding to the woman who held pins between her teeth and appraised me. My father had sent in a fashion consultant and personal designer to ready me for the evening. It sickened me. So much fucking waste. The short, elderly woman with severe spectacles on her nose and perpetually pinched lips, shook her head.

"Not enough room in the shoulders," she groused. "Hard to fit a man like you into a tuxedo, Mister Villanova. Your shoulders are so broad."

Whatever.

"Yeah, do the best you can." Like I gave a fuck.

"Well, on we go then," she said with forced cheerfulness. "You have everything you need. I'll have my team put the finishing touches on this and have it by your door at four o'clock on the nose."

"Thank you," I said with a nod. She took her leave but as the door clicked tight behind her, a voice came over the loud-speaker right near me.

"Dante?" My father's deep, pissed off voice reverberated

around the room.

"Yeah?"

"Come into my office," he growled.

"I'll be there in a minute."

"*Now*." A click sounded. When I was a younger man, I'd feel the fear creeping along my spine at this juncture, and it would be a lie to say I didn't feel a pang of it even now. Mostly what I wanted to do was deck his smug, arrogant face.

Fucking asshole.

I'd be there when I was good and ready. I was twice his size and half his age. What would he do? I pushed aside any thought of what he really *could* do if he wanted to, and put my things away slowly.

What was Gabriella doing right now? Where was she? Was she safe? God, I hated the distance between us. And it was the thought of her that kept my temper in check. I knew that if I appeased him, she'd be safe. If I didn't, and he found her...

I kicked the door of my closet shut and stalked to his office. I knocked hard, relishing the sharp pain I felt along my knuckles when I rapped angrily against the door.

"Come in."

I expected he'd be alone, or with my mother, but he was not alone. Beside him sat Emilio.

I shut the door behind me.

There was no fucking good that would come of this.

"We just wanted a friendly chat before the masquerade, Dante," Emilio said, leaning back in his chair. His hair was slicked back, his eyes calculating slits as he stared at me, the silver scar gleaming from the overhead lights.

He was here for information, and it had to do with Gabriella. I knew it in my gut.

They could cut out my tongue before I'd tell them a fucking thing about Gabriella.

And I knew them. I knew them both. It was a distinct possibility.

"Yeah?" I said, pulling out a chair and taking a seat. I still wore the dress slacks that were custom-made, my shirt unbuttoned at the collar, and I loosened the neck even more. I could feel my blood pressure rising, the heat in my chest consuming me, constricting. I unfastened another button at my neck and tried to look as relaxed as possible.

My father leaned back in his chair, eyeing me. "Where were you last night?" he asked.

I shrugged a shoulder. Why the fuck did he care? "I was with a girl. Spent the night with her. Why?"

He raised a brow. "Why? You need to ask me *why*?"

Though I played it cool, apprehension coiled low in my gut. "I've taken dozens of women to bed. You've never once asked me shit about them. Why would this one be any different?"

Emilio shook his head, his lips quirking. "Don't play us like fucking fools," he growled. "Like you don't know who you are. Like you don't know who *she* is. Like you don't fucking know who her stepmother is."

I fought with everything I had to keep my face impassive, but my fingers curled into fists by my side.

What the *fuck* was he talking about?

"Agatha Madison's fucking step daughter? Really, Dante?" Emilio narrowed his eyes.

No fucking way.

"Way too fucking close to home for it to be coincidence. Yeah, Agatha Madison, the bitch who tried to infiltrate herself as a family princess." His voice dropped to a growl. "I fucking know you're not a dumbass."

Apparently, I was. I schooled my features as I'd been taught to do since grade school, and met his eyes. "What the fuck difference does it make to you who she is? She's just a girl." It was the only lie I'd told.

Emilio leapt to his feet, his chair slamming into the windowsill behind him, coming at me, and my father got to his feet with his arm outstretched to stop him.

"Enough!" he roared.

He was the patriarch of the most powerful mob ring in fucking Vegas, so Emilio sat.

I could hear clock's tick-tock filling the room, as I made myself unclench my fists and breathe deeply in and out, willing myself to calm down. I could see it in my mind's eye, how I'd take Emilio by his motherfucking neck, crack his skull on the edge of the desk, and knee him in the balls. I wanted him to fucking bleed.

I would not give into my baser instincts. I would hold the upper hand, maintain my control, and I would do it by playing my response very, very carefully.

"Agatha Madison. The bitch who blackmailed you into giving her money?" It was a well-kept secret, but one I was privy to.

My father's mistress from long ago.

My father looked at me, his eyes narrowed, as if he were trying to verify my ignorance. "The very same," he said in a low hiss.

I shook my head. "And why would I get a summons here for banging her stepdaughter? What could I possibly do with this knowledge?"

"You fucking idiot," Emilio growled, but my father held up a hand.

"He may have pissed you off, but he's my son, and when you are in my presence you will treat him with respect."

I held Emilio's eyes, not blinking. I wouldn't cave.

My father spoke softly, the deadly calm I hated. "It is too suspicious, Dante. Why would you keep the girl a secret? And why, of all the millions of girls you could have chosen from, did you have to spend the night with *her*? The one affiliated with the woman who tried to tear the family apart? What are your motives here, son?"

My fucking motives? The irony *scalded*.

My *motive* was to hold what was good and pure. To take care of the woman who looked at me as if I hung the moon. And to keep her the fuck away from anything and anyone that would even look at her the wrong way. And here I sat, victim of circumstance, the two of them convinced I was fucking her to undermine the family or some other twisted shit like that.

Jesus Christ.

"I don't have any motives," I said. "I banged her. She was a sweet piece of ass." My hands shook from the lie it hurt to say out loud. I'd told so many lies I'd already paved my road to hell with them, but this one... this one killed me. This one took the one good, pure thing I had and smashed it all to pieces. "I had no motives. Tonight, I go to the masquerade, and tonight, I pick a wife. That's all that matters, right? I choose a bride, I take the throne, Emilio gets second-in-command. You retire in peace and we all live happily ever fucking after. Yeah?"

My father blinked. "Watch your mouth." For a man who took the lives of others without batting an eyelash, he was oddly disturbed by curse words.

I didn't respond, and neither did Emilio.

"So she was just a piece of ass," Emilio said. "You have no plans to see her again?"

"No," I lied, not knowing how I'd get out of this, how I'd save her, near wild with the need to keep her the fuck away from their evil claws.

"She isn't coming tonight?"

I shook my head. "I can't imagine how. She doesn't have

the money or the time to do something like that. She doesn't even know about it."

Their eyes met. Had they detected something in my speech? Did they hear the desperation?

The half-crazed longing?

I unfastened another button at my neck. It felt suddenly too warm in here.

The phone buzzed on my father's desk and he smacked it. "Yeah?"

"Is Dante with you?" My mother.

"He is."

"Are you almost done?"

My father frowned at me, staring across the room before he nodded slowly. "We're done here," he said, hanging up the phone, not bothering to be polite to her.

Was this my future? To be married to a woman I did not love, trapped in a position that forced me to teach people respect and fear?

He looked at me across the room. "I'll take your word for it, son," he said, and as he looked at me a muscle twitched in his jaw as Emilio's eyes focused on me. "And tonight, you'll keep your word. Understood?"

I swallowed. "Of course."

He looked at me for one more moment before he let me go, then he gave me one short nod. "Go, then."

I left, and went to seek my mother. I didn't know how any of this would play out.

But I would do whatever I had to do to protect Gabriella.

---

*A*s it grew darker, the night wearing on, I stared in the mirror, hardly recognizing myself.

I supposed I looked good enough to parade around. Good

enough to find a fucking wife. I fit the part.

I wanted to punch something, break something, watch it splinter beneath my fingers. I needed to find Gabriella, but it would be stupid chasing after her now.

The only way to keep her safe was to keep my distance.

Tonight, I'd play my part and find a girl. I would do whatever they told me to if it fucking killed me.

"Meet me at midnight."

We had a date tomorrow. Jesus. How could I uphold that after all that had gone down?

I held her in my hands, for such a brief time, and now... now I'd have to let her go.

"May I get you anything, Mister Villanova?" Guthrie, my personal assistant, stood in the shadows of my room.

"Get me hard liquor," I said. "In my small silver flask. Something good, something strong, something that'll get me through the night."

I glanced out the window, at the teeming, twinkling lights that highlighted the city, unable to do anything but stare, as I let my mind wander.

I'd tear off the suit and tie and put on my jeans and t-shirt and boots. I'd take nothing but cash and my wallet, and I'd find her. I'd hire someone if I had to but now that I knew her name and the restaurant where she worked, I'd find her. She'd fight me, maybe, but if I told her... if I told her she was in danger, that they could hurt her, that I had enough money for us to leave and never look back... would she go?

Would she trust me?

I closed my eyes, allowing the fantasy to bloom. "I'll go with you, Daddy," she'd say, her beautiful green eyes gazing up at me, so trusting and sweet. And I'd take her. We'd drive until we didn't even know where we were. We'd leave it all behind. We'd find a new home. I'd marry her in a little chapel somewhere, and make her my wife. We'd never come back.

But it was just a fantasy.

They'd find me. They'd find her. And some way or another they'd hurt her.

The door opened and Guthrie handed me my glass and a flask. "Thank you."

My phone buzzed. I clenched my hand around it a moment before glancing at the screen.

My mother.

"It's time, Dante. Come join us, son."

I took another long swig from the flask, the elixir I needed to steel myself for what lay ahead.

"On my way."

I stood with my father, at the head of stairs overlooking the hall. It was ridiculously extravagant, and I smirked in scorn at the frivolity below us. So fucking ironic that the most violent, amoral people in the state could feign such beauty.

Crystal hung from the ceilings, while couples twirled beneath the lights, in step to the full string orchestra dressed in tuxes that played before us. White-gloved waiters and waitresses served cocktails and hors d'oeuvres as I looked on in disdain.

I knew dozens of the women and men who danced before me. Many were money-hungry, greedy, ruthless. I wanted none of them.

I'd give anything to take my girl to a little diner that served French fries on chipped plates with cans of Coke, would give anything for just for a minute with her purity, her innocence, the cleansing wholesomeness of Gabriella.

I watched as a woman most would call gorgeous entered the room on the arm of a tall, darkly handsome man from my crew. She wore an emerald-green gown that fit her well, her full bust nearly spilling over. Her lips were painted red, her hair done up in a fancy, severe up-do that accentuated her high cheekbones. Men turned as she walked on dangerously high stilettos, her hips swaying to the music. I nearly scoffed. Other men found such women attractive. I did not.

I'd seen beauty. I'd tasted beauty. I'd held beauty in my arms.

No other women would turn my head.

"She has a goddamn nerve," my father hissed next to me, and I looked at him in surprise. He pointed a finger with narrowed eyes at a woman I didn't recognize, someone who held the arms of two young women. One was dressed in a flouncy black gown that made her look like some kind of possessed bat, and the other was dressed in a crimson gown, wearing heels that defied gravity. She held her head up with pride as they made their entrance, each holding masks to their faces. I did not need to see beyond those masks to know their eyes were greedy, their mouths pursed or twisted.

"Agatha," my father growled. I looked at him in surprise. Agatha? Gabriella's evil stepmother?

Jesus Christ.

"Why is she here?" I asked, feeling the tension seep into me as my fists clenched by my side and I looked harder in the woman's direction. "What does she want with us?"

My father narrowed eyes before he spoke. "There are many things you do not know, Dante."

What a strange thing to say now.

"That woman and I have a history," was all he said as he continued to stare below. "She's wanted in on the family since before I could remember, and she's done everything in her power to get there. Tonight's no exception. She brought her daughters here because she wants one of them to find *you.*"

My stomach twisted. I felt suddenly sick.

"That's ridiculous," I sputtered.

My father shook his head. "If you knew our history, you'd know just how ridiculous it was." He took a sip from a champagne flute and he looked over the crowd, thereby dismissing the imposter. "I don't care who she is. She's dead to me, as are her daughters."

It wasn't surprising. My father spoke like that often.

I watched as woman after woman filed in the room but I did not take my eyes off of Agatha and her daughters. The room now teemed with women. They were, supposedly, beautiful. But none caught my attention. None were her.

"I'm going to take a walk," I said. "I need some fresh air." The cool metal flask banged against my chest, tucked in the vest I wore, calling to me. I stepped past my father, ignoring the men who stepped aside, his army of bodyguards. He held a hand up, not even looking my way, dismissing them from following me. He knew I'd come back. I had to.

I made my way to the garden, decorated in a white trellis with roses and greens, a beautiful, ornate structure guests walked under to get to the ballroom. To the right sat my mother, her ankles crossed while she watched the arrival of our guests, sipping a glass of wine. When I reached her, she looked up to me and grinned.

She looked regal, almost, the way she held her head high as I approached.

"Dante," she said, inclining her head.

I just nodded back, as she turned to watch the women approach the ballroom. "Does it astound you to know that one of these women is your future wife?" Her voice dropped to a whisper as she continued. "The one you will spend the rest of your life with. The one who will bear your children." She sighed deeply. "I hope fate is good to you tonight, Dante."

Fate would not be good to me.

I shrugged, about to reply, when I saw her, I fucking *saw her,* and my world came to a screeching halt.

She wore the most beautiful blue dress I'd ever seen. It looked like it'd been painted on her, silvers and blues that dipped low in the front revealing her full, beautiful breasts.

I'd buried my face in those breasts. My heart kicked up and my breath hitched.

The dress narrowed at the waist then billowed out in filmy, silvery skirts. Though she wore the signature mask that all guests held to their faces, there was no denying who she was. And it wasn't enough. It wasn't enough to hide her from them, damn it.

What the fuck was she doing here?

"I'll be back," I said to my mother, trying to appear nonchalant, but knowing she wasn't stupid.

If she replied, I didn't hear her, for the blood pounding in my ears prevented me from hearing a thing. If she waved to me, I didn't see her, as I could only see one heartbreakingly beautiful woman in the room, the only one who didn't belong there.

I nodded and waved on autopilot to those who greeted me as I passed, needing to get to her before anyone else did, needing to get her the fuck out of here, but she was headed in the opposite direction.

If she was approached by another man, if anyone ever touched her... I'd have to kill him, and avoiding murder was probably a good thing.

"Excuse me," I said, pushing past a woman who held a glass of wine to her lips, accidentally spilling her wine.

"Hey!" she said, but I couldn't be bothered to stop. I glanced quickly at the spilled wine and when I looked back, Gabriella was gone.

"Sorry!" I yelled over my shoulder. Where was she? Where had she gone? I was torn between wanting to find her, needing to take her someplace safe, and wanting to turn her over my knee and spank her ass for even coming. How *could* she? This was not safe. This was not a place I wanted her to be. Fucking hell, if he ever saw her... if my father knew she was here... But she didn't know, and that was my fault.

I shoved past a couple taking selfies by the garden, and raced past a couple making out by the gazebo. I turned my head to the left and caught a glimpse of silver and blue, but when I raced ahead, it turned out it belonged to someone old enough to be my mother.

I had to find her. Jesus, I needed to find her *now*. And when I did, I'd teach her to stay where she was fucking safe.

I turned the corner by the entrance, and I came to a screeching halt. There she was. There she stood, holding the eye mask tentatively up to her face, but it could not mask her fear. Her innocence. Her purity. I ran as fast as I could, just as her hand went to the doorknob that would take her to the entrance, to where my father stood watching each one of his victims enter.

"Gabriella," I hissed, and I knew she heard me when she froze. She turned to face me, and the mask fell, her mouth opened in surprise, and her brows lifted. I reached her then, snagged her hand and pulled her along with me. "Follow me. Let's go."

She was frozen in place. "Dante?" she whispered.

"Yeah, babe. It's me. Now *move*. You shouldn't be here. Jesus, if he sees you..."

"Who? Why? What's the matter?"

"Jesus, Gabriella," I fumed. "Do what you're fucking told or I swear to God I'll spank your ass. *Move!*"

The threat to spank her seemed to effectively motivate. I tugged, and she ran, but not easily. I glanced down.

"What the fuck are you wearing?"

"Oooh. My slippers. Did you see these? They're custom-

184 • MAFIA DADDY

made, Dante, decorated with *real* silver and *real* diamonds, and one of a kind. They don't fit anyone else because my feet are weirdly tiny, so they had to be adjusted, you know? And they must've cost a mint, but I have no idea—"

"Hush," I hissed, "Tell me later, baby."

I tried to walk as discreetly as possible without arousing suspicion, and she trotted to keep up.

"Well, then," she huffed, "Nice to see you, too."

"It is nice to see you. You look beautiful. Now be quiet, for Christ's sake."

She blinked, but she obeyed, and finally, *finally*, we came to a clearing, out in the back, where the trees covered a vacant patio, and a swing faced out away from the crowd. I brought her to the most private place I could, and when we got there, I pulled her onto the swing to sit. Our chests heaved from running, and I couldn't say anything for a minute while I caught my breath. She finally put her mask down, and grinned at me, and my anger and fear melted away. Her cheeks dimpled, her eyes lit up, and her whole demeanor changed.

God, she was breathtaking. And she was *here*.

"You look stunning," I said, taking her hand and kissing her fingertips. "Amazing."

"Thank you," she whispered. "I... I wasn't going to come. But then Ruby told me you were coming."

Who the fuck was Ruby again? And why the fuck did she know my business? What was this all about?

"She said you would be here, and that helped me make my decision," she said. "I honestly had no interest in coming otherwise."

I looked around me. Didn't look like anyone noticed us yet, but they would. Soon, they'd be looking for me. I wished I could tell her I was glad she came, but I wasn't. I was pissed, and fucking nervous as hell, and I didn't do nervous.

And then she leaned in and looped her arms around my neck, and brushed her sweet cheek against mine. "Are you glad I came, Daddy?" she asked. God, I couldn't send her away. Not now. She continued, her voice wobbling a little. "Do you not want me here? You don't look too happy, and I'm not sure why."

"Baby, listen," I said, burying my face in her sweet-smelling hair, wishing that our circumstances were different, but as she held onto me, something in me shifted.

Why did I have to do what they wanted me to? Why was I here, fucking *hiding* the woman I loved? Did I have no power in all this? Yeah, I didn't want her near them. I wanted to keep her safe, out of their reach, but it was too late for that now.

I made my decision then. I would not be cowed. I would not back down.

They fucking knew who she was. So why would I change who *I* was? She was mine. She was *fucking mine*, and I'd do whatever it took to protect her.

"Of course I'm happy you came, Gabriella," I whispered, holding her close to me, and I knew then, there was no going back. I'd have to tell her. She'd have to know who I was.

God.

"Honey, I have a question for you." I tugged her a bit closer.

"Yes?" she asked, her head cocked to the side.

"Do you know anything about this party tonight?" I asked her. She shook her head slowly, her eyes growing concerned as she looked at me. Her Ruby had been selective then.

"But I... I do know that my stepmother came. That she brought her daughters, and that she did it because she's hoping to get an in with the..." her voice dropped. "The Villanova family." She hadn't put it together yet. Sweet girl. And then she looked at me and her mouth slowly opened, her eyes betraying her fear before fluttering closed as realization dawned on her.

It would've been cute how slow she was to see the truth, if it hadn't been so goddamned tragic.

"You're a Villanova," she whispered. "Dante. Dante Villanova." Her eyes remained closed as she stated my name. "You are the heir to the Villanova throne, aren't you?" she whispered, and her eyes opened and met mine, those innocent, beautiful eyes now damp with tears.

I nodded my head and swallowed hard. "Yeah, baby," I said, not able to tell her anything but the truth. I had to. "That's me."

"Why didn't you tell me?" she choked out.

"I wanted you to know me. The real me. Not the one the media calls ruthless and bloodthirsty."

She swallowed hard, her face paling before she whispered. "Are you, Dante? Ruthless? Bloodthirsty?"

I shook my head. "Bloodthirsty, no. I hate violence, baby. But ruthless? If I have to be, fuck yeah."

Her eyes closed for a brief moment before she opened them again, and lifted her chin, brave and certain. "I don't care."

"You don't care about what?" I asked, grasping her around the waist and tugging her over to me, needing to hold her, needing to know that what we had wouldn't go away because of my fucking family name.

"That you're a Villanova. That you're... one of them. Whether they want to admit it or not, you're a good man, Dante. I know it. I'm a good reader of character, you know," she said with a serious nod of her head.

I could only grin at her.

"Are you, baby?" I asked, dragging my hand from her waist up her slender back, making her shiver before I slowly smoothed my fingers through her beautiful, soft blonde hair, careful not to mess it up. "Then what do you think, Gabriella?" I whispered in her ear. "What's your read on my character? What do you think?"

"You're a good man who loves his family," she whispered. "You are loyal and brave, and fearless. That's not what I think. It's what I *know*. It's what I see. It's what I *feel*."

And I knew then that I loved her, this girl I'd only just met, who'd walked into my life and resurrected the man I once was, the man who'd been mired in a vice so long he hadn't come up for air in fucking decades.

"Although..." her voice trailed off and she worked her lower lip.

"Yeah?"

"Do you, like... really make men... you know..." her voice dropped to a whisper, but she was unable to hide the excitement in her eyes. "Swim with the fishes? For real? Really?"

I barked out a laugh so hard she jumped, literally jumped, right in front of me.

I held her in my arms, pulling her straight to me. "Swim with the fishes," I murmured, my body shaking with laughter.

"I'm serious!" she hissed.

"Listen, Gabriella. You're here tonight, and you're with me. I want to enjoy the time we have here but I need to make sure no one knows who you are. I want to keep you safe. I don't want to talk about what I do or who I am. It's not the time or place, baby."

I noticed the music then, the speakers piping it through the garden, a sweet, hauntingly melodic tune played on the violin. I didn't recognize it, but it spoke to me, and I placed my hand on the small of her back to steady her, to draw her in, so that our bodies were flush against one another. I drew her to her feet, took her hand in mine, nestled my other hand against her hip, and we danced.

We danced in silence, holding each other, as the music

played on. I didn't know how things would play out now that they knew who she was. I had to bring her somewhere safe. But where? How?

"Dante?" she whispered after a few minutes. She trembled a bit, and I wondered if she was cold, but the night was so warm.

"Yes?"

"So if you're like... a Villanova. You're a criminal, huh?"

I would hold nothing back from her.

"Yeah, baby."

We continued to dance in silence for another minute before she spoke again, and this time her voice warbled a bit.

"Would you protect me if anyone tried to hurt me?" I nearly laughed again, but her question was so serious I couldn't do that to her. I hid a smirk by burying my face in her hair, but when I really thought about her question, really contemplated where it came from, I nodded my head, sobering.

"Gabriella, if anyone ever tried to hurt you, they'd have to get through me first. I'd never let anyone touch you. Ever."

We danced a bit, and then, "Would you... kill them? If they tried to hurt me?"

I swallowed, determined not to lie to her. "I try not to kill people, Gabriella."

She had to know this side of me, the ruthless side that lived by another set of laws. I would not hide that from her.

A moment later, her plaintive, sweet voice whispered in my ear again.

"Daddy?"

My body warmed, my eyes briefly shut before I opened them, my cock hard just hearing her call me daddy.

"Here we are."

I smiled. "Here we are," I repeated.

"But...where do we go from here?" she asked.

I didn't have a fucking clue. "I'm not sure, Gabriella. I don't know what we'll do. I do know that tonight, you're here with me. And soon, everyone will know you're mine."

"Everyone?" she asked in a whisper.

We danced on. "I'm not sure how we can prevent it at this point. But we need to be careful with how we approach things. When we go up there, to the ballroom, you put your mask on. Yeah?"

"Uh oh."

"Uh oh what?"

"It's your stern daddy voice."

I smiled, and shook my head. "My what?"

"Your stern daddy voice," she said. "The one you use when you're getting all serious and dominant. I mean not like you aren't always dominant, you know? Don't misunderstand me. I'm not saying you're, like, a wimp or anything. I just mean when you're getting all into commander mode."

I tickled her side and she giggled and snorted up against me.

"All commander mode, huh?" I asked.

"Yep. And your eyes go all stormy and you cross your arms on your chest as if you're ready to fight battle."

God. If she only knew. Still, I couldn't help but smile at her observation.

"Yeah? Then what?"

She ducked her head shyly against my shoulder. "And then you threaten to spank me if I disobey you. At least..." her voice trailed off.

I smoothed my hand over her back, her beautiful, curvy body pushed up against mine. "At least what?"

She leaned in and whispered in my ear. "At least that's how it ends in my fantasy."

My cock lengthened as I held her against me. "It ends with the threat of a spanking?"

"Mmmhmm. Yes. I prefer to end it there because it hurts when you spank me." I pulled her away and her eyes were twinkling. I'd ride this.

"Is that right, little girl? So you don't like when Daddy really spanks you?"

Her pupils dilated and her cheeks flushed. "No," she croaked.

"You're lying," I whispered, tapping her chin with my finger. "Aren't you?"

She swallowed and didn't respond, but I would push this.

"Little girls who lie to their daddies get punished," I said, shaking my head. "Such a shame to have to put a girl in a ball gown over my knee."

She grinned at me and shook her head. "Not a shame at all."

"Then you *were* lying," I said, doing my best to give her the "stern daddy voice."

She bit her lip. "I'm sorry, Daddy. But you're right. I was lying. I love it when you take control." her voice lowered. "When you spank me."

Good, because she had a damn good one coming.

The music stopped and I listened. It was time. I would be wanted up in the main area now, and I'd have to play the part of the gracious host. "I have to get back up to the ballroom," I said. "You remember what I told you. Your mask is on at all times when you're up there. Yeah?"

She nodded. "Yes, Dante."

"Good girl." I pulled her to me, and kissed her forehead, not knowing what would happen next, where we'd go from here. I only knew she was mine, and that I would do anything to keep her safe.

CHAPTER FOURTEEN

I couldn't believe it. I was too stunned, really, to process much at first, but even after I found out who Dante was, I knew I couldn't let this be the end for us.

I didn't have any money. And Dante was the heir to an organized crime ring. How would I reconcile that? What would we do?

But I had to reconcile this. He was the man I'd fallen in love with.

"Always keep your mask on," he said, pulling me along with him. "When we get to the dance floor, I have to play my part for a little while. Stay close, wear your mask, and you talk to no one. Yeah?"

I nodded. "Yes, Daddy."

He was being a little crazy. But, we were talking about a guy who knocked skulls together professionally, so maybe he had a point.

"Let's go," he said, dragging me along with him. When we entered the ballroom, I was momentarily blown away by the sheer opulence, but that's when I saw her. I froze, and even though I held my mask in place, my whole body reacted on instinct. Agatha stood, her two daughters by her side, surveying the room around her with disdain. Her cold, calculating look went from one person to the other, not fully looking at anyone. I hoped she'd glaze right over me, but I couldn't know for sure how she'd react. Dante, of course, noticed my reaction.

He paused, bent down, and whispered in my ear. "What's the matter?"

"She's here," I whispered back, my foot still paused halfway up a stone stair that led to the main hall.

"Who?"

"Agatha," I said with a grimace. "My stepmother. She's here with her daughters. I knew they'd be here, but I didn't know how it would affect me, seeing them like this." I buried my head on his shoulder. "Even with the mask on, what if they recognize me?" I asked fearfully. "She hates me, Dante. She'll see me punished for this, somehow. I know she will. She would be enraged to know I was with you."

"No one is gonna hurt you, baby. I promise you that." He gathered me close, his huge, strong body like a force field against all that would hurt me, and for a moment, I allowed myself to feel his strength, to really embrace him back, my body soft against his. And then they turned to us, people watching him as he walked into the ballroom with me, and I almost lost my nerve. I almost turned and fled. I could hear soft murmurs around us, feel everyone's eyes on us, and the little mask I wore seemed suddenly far too small, like I was grasping a teeny floaty ring in a riptide.

"Smile," he said in my ear. "And keep walking. You'll be fine, baby."

His raspy voice gave me courage and strength, as I held onto him and kept walking to where he led me, and then the orchestra broke into song and he swept me to the side as couples began to dance. My heart stuttered in my chest, my hands shook, and a fine sheen of perspiration dotted my fore-head beneath the mask. I couldn't deal with this. I couldn't handle the pressure. What would Agatha do if she saw me? How would his father handle everything?

He was leading me toward someone who stood in the distance, a beautiful, sophisticated older woman with blonde-gray hair swept up into an elegant up-do. She was beautiful, her gentle eyes troubled as she looked about her. This was a woman who had seen much, but when her gaze rested on Dante, her face lit up. I liked her already.

Anyone who could look at him like that was someone I could love.

She smiled and held her hands out to him as he approached, one protective arm around the small of my back.

"Do what I say, Gabriella. Follow my lead. Understand?"

I nodded. "Yes, of course."

Though the woman smiled benevolently at Dante, her gaze began to flit about the room.

"Dante," she said warmly, putting a hand out that he took and she squeezed. "Where have you been? We've looked everywhere for you. Your father is beside himself."

I felt Dante stiffen next to me. "He'll be fine," he said. "Mom, I want you to meet someone." He turned to me, and his voice hardened. "Do not remove your mask," he ordered, then he took me by the hand and pulled me forward. "Mom, meet Gabriella. Gabriella, my mother, Adele Villanova."

Oh my God. This was his mother. He was introducing me to his *mom*.

She smiled widely at me, and shook my hand, leaning down to whisper in my ear. "I would hug you, Gabriella, but we must be discreet. If he wants your identity hidden, it's for good reason." Then she pulled away, still smiling brightly.

I could only nod. "Pleased to meet you," I said, suddenly wishing the little mask in my hand was a paper bag or something like an invisibility cloak to help me feel less awkward. The hand that held mine grew tighter at the same time Dante said in a low whisper, "He's coming. I'll go to meet him. Mom, you watch her."

And he was gone, quickly whisked away to go see someone. With a quick tug, his mother drew me close to her. She leaned over as a waiter walked by with drinks in long, stemmed glasses, and plucked two of them off the tray. "Here," she said, still smiling, but speaking quietly so that only I could hear her. "Take one. We're going to carry on and speak politely to one another but speak of absolutely nothing. And call me Adele. Okay?" She grinned, then, but it was forced and I could only nod. I took the glass of champagne and swallowed, grateful my mask only covered my nose and eyes, for I needed the liquid courage.

We watched the dancers, the room alight with laughter and music and lights before she got a second drink for me that I drank as rapidly as my first.

"He's going to have him dance with some other women, Gabriella," Dante's mom whispered to me. "Don't let it bother you. It's just part of the game, the way Dante must keep up appearances, okay? None of them mean a thing to him."

I appreciated her kind words. But even her warning did not prepare me for watching Dante take women to the dance floor, one after the other—beautiful, elegant, cultured women. They whispered things in his ear that made him laugh, and he played the part of the gracious host with ease, his eyes not meeting mine once. I knew he had to do this. If he looked at me, others would notice. Still, it stung.

And then she was there, *Agatha*, Elenora on her left and Violet on her right, and they were waiting their turn to dance with Dante.

Nausea clawed at my stomach at the thought of his

strong, powerful hands on either one of them. I hated this. I could not bear to watch. It surprised me how vehemently I reacted to seeing them even close to him, knowing that Agatha's plan was to get one of them into Dante's good graces, and more.

"I need to use the ladies' room," I choked out to his mother, who blinked in surprise.

"Yes, of course," she said. "It's right behind us. I'll follow, and wait for you."

She gestured for me to walk behind the throng of people, to where a hallway brought us to the restrooms. I nodded my thanks to her, and pushed the door open to the ladies' room, taking in deep, cleansing breaths as I made my way to the sink. I looked around me. The vast room adjoined a sitting room with silk-covered seats and large mirrors with gilded frames hanging on the wall. Just beyond where I stood, two women I did not know fixed their make-up in the mirror, but then they left, and I was alone. I needed some cold water, and I couldn't do anything holding the damn mask up to my face. I placed it down, turned on the tap, and splashed a bit of cold water on my face, letting it dribble in my parched mouth, when the door opened. I grabbed at my mask, but it slipped from my hand, crashing to the floor. I couldn't reach it in time. My stomach twisted as I realized I'd shown my face. I picked up the mask and held it in place, but it was too late. When I turned around, Agatha stood in front of me.

At first, her eyes merely registered surprise, before they bled to red hot fury. "You," she said, walking toward me with her index finger pointed directly at me. "*You*!"

And it was in that moment that I really knew how much she hated me, I truly understood that any kindness she'd ever shown me held an ulterior motive. I'd spent the past few years trying to do what my father had asked me to, to take care of Agatha. I'd done what I thought my duty was, devoted myself to the business, even though I had nothing to call my own, not even a friend or a car or a day off to myself.

I'd made a terrible mistake. I'd been played for a fool. And when her eyes met mine, I could feel the rage, see her anger.

"You!" she screamed, her voice ringing with fury. "How dare you come?" she hissed. "You don't belong here. You are nothing more than a whore," she began, when the door to the bathroom swept open and Dante's mother walked in. Agatha turned, pushed past both of us as quickly as she'd come in, and we both stared at the door as it swung shut.

"Are you all right, Gabriella?" she asked, her eyes filled with concern. "That woman looks vaguely familiar to me. I heard her raise her voice, and so I came straight in. Do you know her?"

I stared at the door and nodded my head. "I do," I said, my voice quavering. "She's my stepmother."

Adele's eyes registered surprise. "Oh," she said. "That's a bit... surprising. Why did she look so angry at you?" she whispered.

"Because she hates me," I answered miserably.

She shook her head, dumbfounded, and then she looked down at my hand where I still held my mask. Her eyes gentled and one hand reached for the side of my face, tenderly cupping my jaw. My eyes met hers once more. "And he's right, Gabriella. You are beautiful. I'm honored to see the girl behind the mask. I don't know you, nor do I know how this evening will play out. But I can see it in your eyes, Gabriella. You are good for my son. Only someone who welcomes malice and spite could ever hate a girl like you." She pulled me into a brief embrace. "Now put that mask back on before he sees you without it and loses his *mind*."

And spanks my ass, I added mentally. He'd lose his mind all right.

I obeyed, my hands trembling, as she brought me out to

the ballroom. Something had shifted in the air, then, but I didn't know what yet. Dante was still dancing with one girl after another, but he shook his head as his father said something to him. And before I knew what was happening Agatha stood with her two daughters in front of us. Dante looked aghast at the two of them. I could imagine the man standing next to Dante—the one with the wicked, calculating eyes, but Dante's strong jaw and brow—could only be his father. He shook his head, pointed a finger at Agatha, and her face grew scarlet.

I held on to Adele's hand as I continued to walk. I could see him standing in a sea of faces surrounded by beautiful women who were much more beautiful than I was, and I hated it. At the same time, my breath caught in my throat. What was happening? Agatha was growing more agitated, gesturing now, as Dante's father shook his head. Dante pointed to somebody, snapped his fingers, and before I knew it another woman was in his arms, another woman in the arms of the man that belonged to me. The next thing I know they were dancing. I couldn't bear to watch.

I needed to leave. I needed to get out of there. And then a noise stopped me. The room grew quiet as all eyes turned back to Dante, dancing, and his father facing off with Agatha, who wouldn't leave.

His voice rose so I could hear him clearly now. "You have no business here. I never invited you and you should not be here—you *or* your daughters."

I glanced aside at Adele who stood agape.

"I remember now," she whispered to me, her eyes meeting mine with a question in them, but I had no idea what it was about. "She's the woman. The one my husband had an affair with."

No.

I couldn't even process this as I shook my head, for now

Dante's father had grown livid, gaining the attention of everyone there.

"Did you really think that I would allow you to dance with my son?" he said, a vein pulsing in his neck, his face beet red. The place had grown quiet, as everyone, including me, Adele, and even Dante stared. Agatha first grew pale and then her eyes seemed to pop out of her head, her fists by her side.

"You'd scorn me in front of a ballroom full of people?" she hissed.

"I don't know why you think that I would allow you anywhere near my son," said his father. "I told you never to set foot near my family. Everything I gave you was so that you'd stay away. Leave. *Now*."

Dante released the woman he danced with and stepped toward his father. I didn't hear what he said, but I heard his father's response.

"Stay out of this," his father barked, turning toward Dante, and effectively turning his back to Agatha. He snapped his fingers at a line of men dressed in suits, and pointed to Agatha. "Take her away, and her daughters, too, and see they never come back."

Agatha would not go quietly. Women screamed as she lunged at Dante's father, grabbing a nearby champagne flute and throwing it fully at his face, glass and all, the flute smashing up against him and mercifully not breaking until it hit the floor. I screamed. Adele screamed. But the men near Dante's father were already moving. They must've been his bodyguards, the men who would protect him, the army that was sent to defend the king.

As they drew weapons, several things happened at once. Dante turned to *me*, running straight toward me, as Adele pulled me to the floor. And as I fell down, his large arms held me, dragging me to safety, and I heard Agatha's shriek.

"You've kept me away from your precious wife all these

years. She could never know you had a *mistress*. You bought everything you gave me so she wouldn't know. And now you would deny me the one thing I want? Then fuck you! Take your money, everything that you've given me, and go to hell."

I couldn't see much from my position but feet scrambling. I heard more shouts, and then Dante's full body was atop mine as shots rang out. He pushed me down so hard my head hit the floor and his voice hissed low, "Stay still, Gabriella. Don't move until I tell you."

I could only nod, as more shots rang out, screams escalated in volume, and utter chaos reigned above me. I stayed there until he finally whispered, "You need to get out of here. You're going with people who work for me. They will take care of you." He turned to a man with skin as dark as night.

"Take her to the secured room." I didn't want to go without him. I didn't want to go *anywhere*. What had happened? Was everyone okay? I turned to look at Dante but he only shook his head and then strong hands held me, half dragging me to an exit. A large man with a shaved head brought me to a room so small it looked like a sort of cell. I wondered what happened in this room, what sort of things they did? Was this where they would take people to interrogate them? Did they torture people to extract information from them?

Who was Dante, really? And how would things ever be the same between us?

I stayed in the room for what felt like hours but probably was no more than thirty minutes before the door opened and a very tired-looking Dante entered. He scrubbed a hand across his forehead, and his eyes shut momentarily before they met mine. When he looked at me he drew in a breath and sighed. "Gabriella, are you okay? Baby, did they hurt you?"

I only shook my head in silence. I didn't know what to say.

Finally, in a voice that didn't sound like it belongs to me, I asked, "Dante, is everyone okay?"

He pulled me to him, his hand on the small of my back, and held me for moment before he spoke. "My mother's in the emergency room. A bullet grazed her in the shooting. She's the only one that matters."

The hair on my arm rose. "And what about everybody else? Was anybody else hurt?"

His gaze pulled away from mine for moment and he swallowed hard. "Yeah, baby," he said somberly. "My dad didn't make it. I don't know what happened. Nobody does, and we won't know what happened until we see the footage. But it looks like Agatha may have shot him."

"She shot him?" I gasped. "Oh God, no!"

"He may have accidentally been shot by one of his guards when she grabbed a gun and they fired. But it's hard to tell, Gabriella. My father was a man with many enemies. If anyone here saw the chance to hurt him they would have."

"Dante," I choked out, placing a hand on his cheek and gently tipping his face so that his eyes met mine. "I am so sorry."

He laughed mercilessly, a sad, heartbreaking laugh that made me want to cry. "You have no idea. You don't know what this means now. I was next in line, Gabriella. *Me*." He shook his head. "I'm the new head of the Villanova family. And now I need to send you home and you need to pretend you never met me."

My throat felt tight, my skin icy, and I could hardly speak. My voice shook as I tried. "That's... ridiculous," I said. How could I ever forget that I met him? "What does you being the leader have anything to do with us?" He shook his head and released my hand.

"I have something else to tell you," he said, not meeting my eyes. "Agatha is gone. She was shot, and not by accident. Your sisters are being taken to the hospital, but I don't know if their injuries are life-threatening or not. The next few days things are going to be very tricky for us. I need you to lay low. And for God's sake, Gabriella, do what I tell you." He stood and didn't look at me as he marched to the door. "And I'm telling you, now it's time to go home."

I left in a sort of stupor. I didn't know where I was going or who I was with but I knew that my life was about to change. He'd sent me away.

There would be no more midnight meetings, no more trysts. No more moonlight kisses or whispered promises.

When a huge limo pulled up to take me anywhere I wanted to go, I didn't give them directions to the cramped apartment I'd shared with Agatha and my step sisters. Instead, I gave them the directions to Ruby's. The man at the door recognized me and didn't say anything to the men who flanked my sides as he buzzed me up.

"Is everything ok?" the doorman asked. I only shook my head.

No. Nothing's okay. Just take me to Ruby. How could anything be okay? Dante is gone. Agatha betrayed my father, and she's gone now, too.

And as I walked to Ruby's a sort of despair welled up inside me. Where would I go? What would I do? I didn't know.

I didn't know what would happen when I saw her. But I knew that if I said I needed help Ruby would do the best she could to help me. I was like a daughter to her. And she was so very good to me. I needed someone who understood me.

I walked instinctively, just knowing that at the end of my journey would be someone who would understand, someone who would help me move on to the next stage of my life.

When we got to the door, she asked who was there.

"Ruby?" I asked, my voice unnaturally high and tight. "It's me, Gabriella. Please let me in."

She opened the door and I fell into her home as if I couldn't hold myself up any longer.

"Oh, Gabriella. What happened? Tell me. Are you okay? Did he hurt you?" I fell into her arms and burst into tears. She led me to her couch and held me, patting my back and hushing me.

The very thought of him hurting me. "No! No, he didn't. Ruby..."

"Where are your shoes? Honey, who hurt you?"

I didn't even realize I didn't have my shoes on. I had to have lost them when they pulled me away.

"Ruby, I don't know what happened," I sniffed. "Agatha is dead. Dante's father is dead. And Dante is now the new leader of the Villanova crime family."

CHAPTER FIFTEEN

Two weeks later

$\mathcal{I}$ sat by my mother's bedside. She had been released from the hospital the week prior, and the past two weeks had been an absolute blur.

We buried my father. And even though my family didn't agree, I paid for the burial service for Agatha. I sent money so we would cut ties entirely. I wondered if Gabriella would show, but she didn't. I was sort of proud of her. I didn't blame her.

She'd left Ruby's, but I hadn't given anyone instructions to track her, though it killed me.

"And now," I said to my mom, "we put the pieces of the puzzle together."

"I knew he'd had an affair with that woman—I saw her once, though your father never knew. But I had no idea just how horrible she was. She was married to Reginald Madison, and I always knew that he had somebody else," she said. "I never dreamed it was that horrid woman. He was the one that betrayed your father."

"No," I said.

Her eyes widened, but she said nothing. I shook my head. "I've been digging around, asking questions. Reginald Madison never betrayed Dad. Dad agreed to Agatha's demand to kill Reginald so she could have the restaurant and all the money to herself."

She looked away.

I looked out the window and wondered what my options were.

"You've lost so much, Dante. I think it's time that we make some serious decisions."

I turned and looked at my mother, someone who had seen the darkest side of things. "I think it's time for you to move on," she said.

I looked at her. What did she mean?

"Leave, Dante. I want you to leave, and never come back."

My throat felt oddly constricted.

"You don't need to be tied down here anymore. And this isn't who you *are*. You don't revel in the power like they do. You despise it. You've been given a gift, son. Find her. And make a new life for yourself."

All this time I'd thought it was in my family's best interest to carry on the torch, to lead the family, to be the one responsible for everything.

Now my father was gone. Gabriella was gone.

"What will you do without my protection?" I asked. My mother smiled a slow, sad smile. "There are many things you don't know, Dante. And one of them is that I am not hurting for money. I inherited a good deal from my father that I've put aside. You and I will find our ways. And now the opportunity has come." She smiled. "Give the family power to Emilio. He'll love it. And then change your name, son. Move away."

I swallowed hard. "I'm calling a meeting," I said. "It's time that I had a very serious conversation with my cousin. All this time the only reason why I stayed is because I thought that you needed me. That you needed my protection."

She shook her head. "I don't need you to protect me. The only thing I need now is knowing that my son was released of the burden he inherited." She's smiled then, the first real smile. "Dante, we have no obligation to the family anymore. Your cousin will agree to this. He gets all the power." She shook her head. "That's all he wanted from the very beginning."

We sat in silence for a few moments before she said, "Where is Gabriella? Have you seen her since the night of the incident?"

I looked out the window and didn't answer. Of course I had. I'd watched her from a distance. I knew that she sold what little she had and left, thanks to Ruby's help, then paid off her bills and moved to California.

"Do it, Dante. Find the girl. Don't let her get away."

I took a deep breath, pulled out my cell phone, and tapped the button. Emilio answered on the first ring.

"Call a meeting," I said. "Call the entire family. I want everyone there."

———

*W*e sat around the long table all of us seated in silence. It used to remind me of a table from Camelot, where the Knights of the Round Table sat, but I knew better now. These were not men who were brave and filled with valor. Though there were times when we saw glimpses of bravery and selflessness, their real motivations were far different.

All eyes looked to me as I cleared my throat and looked around the room. "Thank you all for coming. My father would appreciate this. And I tell you now that I appreciate your loyalty and service to the family." There was a decided shift in the room as all eyes looked to me. They knew I had something important to say. "With the death of my father and recent events, I feel it's time for me to step down from my role, and I'd like to ask Emilio to take over the responsibilities. So I ask you now, in front of the entire family. Emilio, are you prepared to be the leader?"

Emilio's eyes lit as if I had just handed him a winning lottery ticket. "Of course," he said. "Once more I'd like to offer my condolences to you and your mother. And I think you've made the right choice."

I knew he was full of shit but I let him say it anyway. The rest of the meeting went on in a blur. I swore him in, as was our custom, and vowed that I would never betray the family secrets. He clapped me on the back and wished me well. We both knew what he meant. Go, and never come back.

I left that meeting a free man, the burdens of the family no longer on my shoulders. Now all I had to do was find her. I went back to my room and held the little box in my hand, the box with the custom-made shoe that would only fit her.

I didn't know where she was. I didn't know where I would find her. I didn't even know that if I found her she would take me back. But I had to try.

I took off my shirt and tie and hung them up in my closet. I slid into a worn pair of jeans and a comfortable t-shirt for the first time since my dad passed away. Then I got on my bike and I drove, drove until I got to Ruby's place. When she answered the door, I held up the tiny, glittery shoe. "Help me find her, Ruby."

CHAPTER SIXTEEN

I took off my apron and hung it up on a little hook by the espresso machines. I'd gotten a job as a barista on the West Coast, and I enjoyed the hell out of it. I had a flexible schedule, and a boss that believed in vacation time. I felt as if I've been freed from the slavery I had been imprisoned in, and I did it with the knowledge that my dad would've been happy for me. If he knew the truth, he wouldn't have wanted me to stay behind.

But I wasn't at peace. There was only one person I looked for every time I opened up the coffee shop. Anytime I heard a motorcycle go by, I would look wondering if he'd come for me. Had he found me?

He had a family to take care of, huge responsibilities now that his dad was dead. And I didn't fit in that line of responsibilities. How could his mother ever look at me knowing that I was the stepdaughter of the woman who'd had an affair with her husband?

Sighing, I punched out and left for home. My shift was over, and it was time for me to head back to the studio apartment I'd rented north of the city.

I smelled like coffee, and I needed to shower, I was hungry, but it was still so much better than what I'd had before.

I could've taken a taxi or a bus or something, even gotten a car of my own, but I didn't want to. I liked walking. It reminded me of how I'd met Dante.

My cell phone rang, and I picked it up without looking at the caller ID. He didn't have my number so it wouldn't be him.

"Hello?"

"Where are you, honey?" It was Ruby checking in as she always did.

"I'm just going for a walk."

"It's late, Gabriella. You have to be careful. It's time for you to go home, now. Why don't you get a cab or something?"

"I don't want to."

"Stubborn girl. I had a visitor today."

"Did you?" I said, schooling my features even though she couldn't see me. "And who might that be?"

"A gentleman caller. He wanted to know if I knew where you were."

My heart kicked up a beat and my mouth grew dry. He still cared.

"And did you tell him?" I asked, my voice breathless now, part of me hoping that she'd said no and part of me hoping that she said yes.

Please, please tell me that you told him where I was.

"I did. And I'm not sorry that I did. I think that you're being stupid and foolish not getting back together with him. He needs you, and you need him. We know that you're not going to bring anybody down. You couldn't, any more than the sun could set at noon or rise at midday. It's not going to happen."

"Well," I said. "I suppose that depends on if you were in Antarctica or Alaska. I don't know, I have to look up my geography or something, but I'm pretty sure—"

"Gabriella!" she interrupted.

Right then, I heard it the distance. The rumble of a motorcycle, and not just any rumble. I knew from the moment I heard it, it belonged to him. My heartbeat kicked up. I looked around wildly for a place to hide which didn't even make sense. I saw nothing, though. I didn't know where to go or what to do so I stood there looking around me, and Ruby said, "He's coming, Gabriella, and so help me God you'd better be there when he does."

She ended the call. My hands shook. The sky rolled with thunder and I felt it in my bones, something incredible was going to happen.

For a split second, I fretted that maybe the motorcycle belonged to somebody else, but soon as the rider came into my vision, I knew that it was *him*. My Dante.

And he was coming for me.

He pulled over to the side of the road, took off his helmet, and it was *him* in all his beautiful, badass glory. He smiled at me, and his eyes held sad secrets, but something else now. Hope?

I knew then that I had to talk, that I had to say something brilliant, but I had nothing. I frowned at him. "What took you so long? My flip flop broke." He looked down at my sneakers and shook his head. "And do you happen to have a space on the back of your bike for me?"

He grinned. "Only if you promise not to get off."

Placing the kickstand down, he made his way over to where I stood, shaking in anticipation, my throat clogged with tears. "I won't get off," I whispered in a shaky breath.

When he reached me, he bent down, put both arms

around me, and lifted me straight into the air. I wrapped my legs around his strong back as he cupped my ass and kissed me—a deep, possessive, heated kiss that told me he missed me. I let myself go. I could, now that I was with him. He held me and we kissed like people who love each other should—as if nothing would come between us again. A kiss that said *I love you,* and *I miss you,* and *Don't ever leave me again.*

Finally, our lips parted and I put my head on his shoulder as he held me close, the tears still flowing. "I missed you so much, Dante. I waited for you. And I know after all that waiting that I love you." I cried freely now. It felt good to say it. "I love you, Dante." He patted my back and rocked me a little.

When he spoke, the familiar rasp made me feel warm inside, like someone had just lit a fire in a chilled room, the warmth spreading from my belly to the rest of my body. "I love you, too, Gabriella. And no matter what, I won't let anyone or anything come between us. You're mine, and you always will be. I love you." "Time to get you alone, babe. It's been too long." And he helped me on the back of his bike. I hugged him from behind, my little arms barely reaching around his huge body, but I had to hold him tight.

It was him. My Dante. He'd come for me.

---

*D*ante wrote the last month's check for my apartment, and slid it into my landlord's snail mail box with a Post-It note that said, "This is the last month's rent. I'm moving."

He called movers to come just like that.

Then we got a hotel. We'd spent so many nights at hotels it seemed like it was our thing. He got the swankiest hotel at a place I'd never been. But he said that it would be the last one for a very, very long time. I liked that. I didn't much care where we moved now as long as I was with him.

"Let's go far away," he said. "Forget about the West Coast. Let's go get a cabin in Maine." I laughed outright at that. It seemed so random, and yet so perfect. It was exactly what I wanted, a remote location far away from the memories that we had in Vegas. Someplace new where we would make our home. Someplace where we could... God willing... raise children. Make a family.

"I'd like that," I said. "I could do things, like, you know, can tomatoes and make my own soap and hang out laundry on lines and make bread and stuff."

"Just because you live in Maine you don't have to be a homesteader or something," he said. "But that's okay if you really want to. I don't really give a damn what you do as long as you're with me."

"Well, princess," he said, sitting me on a chair as he removed a shoe from a shelf. "If the shoe fits..." As he drew closer, sparkles glinted in the light. They were my shoes from the ball, the very ones decorated in diamonds and silver, tiny enough to fit my feet.

My mouth fell open in shock. "Oh my God," I laughed. "It fits perfectly. Do you have the other one somewhere?"

He nodded, his eyes twinkling. "I do."

"Well, I bet these are worth a mint," I said, but he shook his head.

"Likely, but we keep the shoes. I don't ever want to forget this moment, okay?" he asked, as he pulled something else out of his pocket.

I stopped breathing as he opened the black velvet box and took out a large oval-shaped diamond set in gold. "Will you marry me, Gabriella? Make my dreams come true? Let me be your Prince Charming?"

I grabbed him around the neck and squeezed so hard he wheezed a little. "Oh my God. Of course! Yes, yes, *yes!*"

He took me in his arms then and held me close, breathing into my ear before he kissed me, "And they lived happily ever after."

THE END

Dungeon Daddy: A Rapunzel Adult Fairy Tale
Chapter one

DUNGEON DADDY CHAPTER ONE

Ryder

I drove with one eye on the time and the other on the road ahead of me, picking up speed. I'd gotten stuck in traffic on the way home from New York, having checked out a new venue for a new club I planned to open. I was doing a demonstration tonight in the dungeon. My nerves were fraught with equal part excitement and raw energy, the way I always felt before I scened.

A pop sounded, my car swerved and bucked, and I screeched to a halt.

Fuck.

"What the hell was that?" I muttered to myself, slowed the car, and navigated it to the side of the road. Swearing under my breath, I parked and got out to assess the damage.

I whistled to myself.

"For Christ's sake." I had no patience for inefficiency. Not only was it too damned dark to change a tire, but the side of the road was little more than a strip of gravel, and safety was an issue. I yanked open the door to my retrieve my phone, then dialed Seth, but the call wouldn't send.

"Stuck in goddamned Hicksville."

I kicked the damaged tire and swore. I was used to giving commands and being obeyed, and hated losing control of a situation. I expected my employees to show on time, and always held myself to the same standards.

Ahead of me loomed nothing but miles of dim streetlights illuminating the two-lane road I'd driven alone on for the past hour. I'd have to change the tire in the dark.

I flipped open the hatch and grabbed the bag and spare, kneeling in the blackness beside the blown tire, feeling for what I needed, then swore aloud again.

The spare was flat.

"Fuck," I muttered under my breath. I had no idea how far I was from the nearest cell phone signal, or even how far I was from civilization.

I walked for a few miles in the direction of town, looking for a road sign, but saw nothing until I came to a cluster of trees on the side of the road. Something glimmered behind the trees, catching my attention. Squinting, I tried to see beyond them, but all I could see was a distant light.

Someone lived just beyond the trees.

As I walked toward it, the light grew brighter, glowing yellow in the dark night sky. A mile or so ahead stood the silhouette of a house lit by the light of the moon, one light shining in an upper window, a wrought-iron fence surrounding the perimeter. The hair at my neck pricked, my senses warning me that something was wrong, that danger loomed ahead, but I wouldn't turn away. I'd learned to handle fear.

I slowed as I drew closer, not knowing what or who to expect, when a shadow crossed the lighted window. I froze and squinted, holding my stance but I was too far to really see anything.

I crept closer. I could see a two-car garage on the side of the house, to the left of that a small, kidney-shaped pool, and what looked like a garden behind that. It was too dark to see more.

Where was the front door? And how would I get past the gate? I looked back in the direction of my car, abandoned some miles behind me. Somehow, I had to get the people who lived here to help me, then get the fuck out.

As I walked toward the gate, it swung open ominously. Someone had forgotten to lock it.

I headed for the entryway, my senses tingling as if someone watched me. The feeling was so strong, I swiveled my head around, but saw nothing but darkness. Walking up the steps, I pushed the doorbell and heard the resounding ring inside. A full minute passed. I pushed it again, wondering if the occupants were home or asleep, when I saw movement again in the upstairs window. I squinted my eyes and looked harder. Two sliding glass doors stood beyond the balcony. Walking over to the side so I could get a better look, once more a shadow flashed by the window, and then it reappeared.

What the fuck?

By now, I was getting annoyed. I needed someone to open the damn door.

I pushed the doorbell one more time, then, just because I wanted to pound something with my fist, I knocked on the door again. "Hey! I just need to use your phone." Nothing.

I looked back up to the window, and caught a glimpse of a curvy figure, and long, flowing hair. She kept herself back in the shadows, only peeking through the very corner of the window.

"Hello!" I yelled, frustration mounting by the minute. I

whipped my cell phone out of my pocket and tried to tap it again, to no avail. Not only had the signal bars dimmed, but the screen now bore an "X" across the notifications panel, barring any possibility of connection.

Shaking my head, I walked toward the road again. Just before I left, I cast one last glance over my shoulder. This time, there was no meek shadow, but the full profile of a woman standing in the middle of the window, staring down at me.

I waved my hands frantically. "Hey! Can you open the door?" I asked. A split second later the woman turned and I heard a plaintive scream. She fell back, as if yanked from behind, then vanished.

My pulse spiked.

Someone had hurt her.

I raced to the house, as I looked for a way to get up to her. She was at least three stories up, and though there was a balcony outside her window, there was no obvious way up, but her window was above a small, fenced-in garden and the fence would give me some leverage.

I scaled the fence and launched myself to the first level alcove hanging beside the house. Heaving myself up, I pushed myself to stand on a flower box outside a window, hoping it would bear my weight. I only needed to leap a foot and a half to grab the rail of the balcony. Pulling myself up, I got to the ledge, my muscles aching from the strain, but adrenaline pumping.

Seconds later, I lifted my body onto the small balcony, and shoved the sliding door open. To my relief, it opened easily. I glanced inside the room, looking for a sign of the girl, but I could see nothing. Had someone taken her? If I yelled they'd hear me, and could hurt her... I had to help her. I stepped inside, but as soon as my feet hit the floor, a blood-curdling scream met my ears. "Trespasser!"

I turned to face the person yelling at me, seconds before something huge and solid loomed in front of me. I saw a flash of silver just before something whacked the side of my head, and I fell to the ground, unconscious.

Read *Dungeon Daddy.* Now live!

A note from the author

.

Thank you for reading *Mafia Daddy: A Cinderella Adult Fairy Tale!*

Are you interested in a **FREE READ?** <u>Sign up here!</u>

What to read next? Here are some *other titles you may enjoy*.

ABOUT THE AUTHOR

Jane is a bestselling erotic romance author in multiple genres, including contemporary, historical, sci-fi, and fantasy. She pens stern but loving alpha heroes, feisty heroines, and emotion-driven happily ever afters. Jane is a hopeless romantic who loves the ocean, her houseful of children, her awesome husband, chocolate, coffee, and sexy romance.

You can stalk Jane here!

Web page: http://www.janehenryromance.com

Amazon author page

Goodreads

Author Facebook page

Twitter handle: @janehenryauthor

Instagram: https://www.instagram.com/janehenryauthor

Don't forget your BONUS EPILOGUE!

OTHER TITLES BY JANE YOU MAY ENJOY:

Contemporary fiction

The Billionaire Daddies Trilogy

Beauty's Daddy: A Beauty and the Beast Adult Fairy Tale

Dungeon Daddy: A Rapunzel Adult Fairy Tale

The Boston Doms

My Dom (Boston Doms Book 1)

His Submissive (Boston Doms Book 2)

Her Protector (Boston Doms Book 3)

His Babygirl (Boston Doms Book 4)

His Lady (Boston Doms Book 5)

Her Hero (Boston Doms Book 6)

My Redemption (Boston Doms Book 7)

Begin Again (Bound to You Book 1)

Come Back to Me (Bound to You Book 2)

Complete Me (Bound To You Book 3)

Bound to You (Boxed Set)

Sunstrokes: Four Hot Tales of Punishment and Pleasure (Anthology)

A Thousand Yesses

Westerns

Her Outlaw Daddy

Claimed on the Frontier

Surrendered on the Frontier

Cowboy Daddies: Two Western Romances

Science Fiction

Aldric: A Sci-Fi Warrior Romance (Heroes of Avalere Book 1)

Idan: A Sci-Fi Warrior Romance (Heroes of Avalere Book 2)